The Trelanton Tales

SIMON PEEL

The Maid of Trelanton and Deep Secrets first published 2013 by Silver Stream Press

Seagull's Exile first published 2014 by KDP

This edition published December 2014

Copyright © 2014 Simon Peel

Editor: Jamie D Rose

Cover art by Juliette Dodd

All rights reserved.

All characters and events portrayed in this book are fictitious. Any resemblance to actual persons living or dead is strictly coincidental.

This literary work may not be reproduced or transmitted in any form or by any means, including electronic or photographic reproduction, in whole or part without express written permission from the copyright holder.

ISBN-10: 1503068161
ISBN-13: 978-1503068162

For Morgy and Juliette

CONTENTS

Foreword

1	THE MAID OF TRELANTON	1
2	DEEP SECRETS	33
3	SEAGULL'S EXILE	91
4	APPENDIX: THE MERMAID GUIDE	161

Acknowledgements

FOREWORD

These three stories were previously published separately, and only in the electronic domain. This is the first time they have been available in print. Although they are presented here in the order in which I wrote them, they can be read out of order with no confusion to the reader. Each works as a self-contained story. In addition, as the world of the merfolk has grown more complex, I have included a handy reference guide in the appendix to help readers keep track of who is who and where is where, and offer the odd tidbit of extra information.

THE MAID OF TRELANTON

When you are sitting on the beach, looking out at the sea on a clear day, it's easy to see right away how the earth is round. Though the horizon stretches like a flat line, when you watch ships sail away they will appear to sink below the dividing line between sea and sky. The hull going first, then the mid parts, then the tip of a sail, or chimney, last of all. I used to often think of that when I looked out to sea, and it was a reminder of how well we humans understand the world we inhabit—its movements and rhythms, its natural laws, and how we are the only animal with the capability to dominate the rest.

Now, when I look out to sea, I don't think about any of that.

It's all changed for me—not in a way that spoils it, far from it—but in the way a mirror moves to show you a new view, even though you are standing in the same place. But let me go back to before that time, when I was concerned with other things.

The date was late April and it was a working day much like any other. Rob Cherryson and I toiled in the anechoic chamber at Mayfield Labs, calibrating the sensors that we'd be using for some vibration tests. It was tedious work, though important if we were to get accurate results from our experiments. The poor ventilation in the chamber made me sweat slightly.

"So did you get much sleep last night, Jon?" asked Rob with a wink. I shook my head. The dark circles around my eyes betrayed my tired state.

"Toby's very loud when he's hungry. Even when a feed is just moments away, those are very *long* moments at three in the morning."

Rob laughed. "That's why I'm not gonna have any kids myself. Can't do without my beauty sleep." Still grinning, he bent to make an adjustment to a sensor plate. While becoming a father for the first time a month ago was incredibly rewarding, it brought with it challenges to be lived through. Anna worked hard as his mother. She would wake to feed Toby whenever he cried at night, ending up with even less sleep than me. She slept with Toby in our bed not only for convenience of feeding but also to help him feel safer and less isolated at night. The spare room had become my temporary sleeping place, as Anna feared with all three of us in the bed I would roll over and crush the little fellow.

The day wore on, my head began to ache, my eyes and throat felt dry, and when the time came to put down screwdrivers and leave the oppressive airless chamber until the next day, I felt quite relieved.

"Sweet dreams then, Dr Moore!" said Rob jovially, as he locked the lab door behind us and headed to his car. The fresh air in the car park cooled my face and I savoured the sensation. As I started the engine of my own car, I decided to take a little detour on the way home. Trelanton Cove lay only half a mile from the lab and I had no need to hurry. Taking the unmarked lane branching off the main road, I followed the winding track towards the north coast. Within minutes I had parked the car near the path leading down to the little bay, and was picking my way down among clumps of thrift until I reached the sandy beach itself. Trelanton was typical of Cornish coves—a small recess cut into low cliffs, with an outcrop of rocks at one end protruding like a natural pier at low tide. A light breeze blew in from the sea and I breathed deeply. Peace presided here with no other people to be seen, and I strolled from one end of the cove to the other then turned and followed my footprints back again. My headache began to lift and the tension in my body to ease. After a while with my own thoughts, I climbed the path back to my car and drove the half-hour journey home.

Coming in to the hall, I could hear Toby crying in the kitchen. I went through to see him, cuddled in Anna's arms but red-faced and wet-eyed.

"Hey there, Toby, what's the matter?" I said soothingly, reaching out to take him from my obviously stressed wife. I lay him against my shoulder and stroked his back, but he continued to snuffle.

"I think he's got colic," Anna said. "He's been crying for the last hour. Nothing's helping him. Oh for heaven's sake, Jonathan, don't hold him like that! You'll make him worse!" She snatched the again-wailing baby from off my shoulder and held him on his side against her body. The cries didn't diminish.

"Sorry, Anna, I was only trying to help. It looks like you've had a tough day. Why not sit down. I'll make you a coffee. Perhaps if you're still he might settle down a bit?"

"No, you're meant to move them about if they have colic," she huffed, pacing up and down the kitchen. Her dark, curly hair looked tousled and frizzy, and she gave the impression of needing proper rest. Tired though I was, Anna looked worse. My offer of childcare refused, I went to have a shower.

* * * *

A week or two later I was working on a particularly difficult piece of the experiment late one morning. As before, I was in the anechoic chamber, lying on my back to adjust a sensor plate beneath the metre-wide piece of ceramic we were testing. I had hardly any room and the stuffy air closed around me uncomfortably. I didn't have Rob to help me and again I felt a tension headache beginning to form. I realised that trying to do precision work was impossible feeling as I did; I needed to take some time out. Leaving a note for Rob in case he should return, I went for an early lunch break. I remembered the refreshing tranquillity of Trelanton Cove and thought I'd walk there this time. The sunshine brought out the beauty of the landscape and I enjoyed the hike to the beach. When I arrived, there were a couple of people playing with a dog, which frolicked in the waves, but there was nobody else around. The tide was out and I decided to walk along to the rocky promontory at the other end of the cove. Halfway across the sand, the dog came racing up to me and bounded about, holding a stick in its mouth and wagging its tail furiously before galloping back to its owners, who waved cheerily as they passed in the opposite direction. By the time I reached the rocks, the dog was eagerly climbing the path to the top of the cliff, pursued by its masters, who shouted for it to heel.

I clambered up the rocks and outwards along the natural groyne they made, dividing the cove from a smaller, less accessible bay on the other side. Kittiwakes nested on the cliff on that side, safe from disturbance by humans or other predators. Other than from the sea, passing across the rocks as I had was the only access to this little beach. A few isolated rocks stuck up like tiny islands just beyond the wash of the waves. I had been looking at these for a moment or two before I suddenly noticed the presence of another person. A woman lay on the flattest of the rocks—or at least leaning across them— her legs appeared to be in the water and she rested her head and upper body face down on the rock. It was an unusual place to swim, with the turbulent currents around the cliffs, and an even odder place to try and sunbathe. The sun's warmth was tempered by the splashing of the water, still chilly at this time of year. Even stranger, the woman seemed to be naked—or at least topless. Perhaps that was why she'd chosen such an isolated spot. It made me feel a little awkward and intrusive. I looked back at the beach I'd come from to see if there were any other people there. The couple with the dog were visible in the distance at the top of the cliff and wouldn't be able to see her from where they were.

But when I turned back to look again, she had gone. I couldn't see her anywhere in the sea and she certainly hadn't come out of the water onto the beach. Apart from some gulls bobbing on the waves, I saw nothing. After resting there on the rocks for a few minutes longer, I began the walk back to the lab.

For the rest of the day I couldn't shake the thought of what I'd seen. I began to worry the woman was dead or injured—what if she had been washed up from a ship then a wave had snatched her corpse back under when I wasn't looking? Or even worse, what if she was still alive and being helplessly thrown about by the sea? She surely wouldn't last long. When Rob returned in the afternoon, I mentioned the incident to him.

"Hmm, I'm sure it's nothing to worry about," he said. "She probably just swam away and you didn't spot her. If you're really worried, maybe call the coastguard. If any swimmers have gone missing or people fallen off ships, they'll know, right? Was she a hot chick, by the way?" I ignored him.

I took his advice and rang the coastguard station. They'd had no reports of any ships sinking or losing crew and no swimmers adrift that they knew of, but they'd send a boat out to look, just in case. That eased my mind, knowing if she had been in trouble, at least I'd alerted the authorities. I kept a close eye on local news reports in the following days, but saw no mention of floating corpses recovered from the sea. I began to forget about her, except for when Rob made tasteless jokes about 'Trelanton nudist beach'.

The following week I went down to the beach again before driving home after work. Anna and I had argued that morning over her accusation that I was useless at feeding Toby with a bottle and it should be left to those with the natural equipment to do so. I just wanted to do something to help bond with our son and at the same time give Anna a break from the demand feeding. I felt rather snubbed by her attitude and wanted to compose myself before coming home. The tide was out again and once more I was alone on the sand. I trudged across to the rocks again and climbed to the vantage point I'd had before. I hoped I wouldn't find a semi-eaten body with seagulls pecking at its eyes, but in the back of my mind I did consider the possibility.

And there she was. Not dead—but again lying on her front on the flat rock in the early evening sun, half in, half out of the waves, which were a little gentler today. And this time I could see her face, as her head was turned towards me—her eyes closed. She had the most beautiful face, with very long, dark hair lying in wet strands across her back and around her shoulders. Like before, she wore nothing on her upper body. I felt a little embarrassed looking at her while she remained unaware of me, but I couldn't help it. It's not in my nature to openly ogle attractive women on the beach, but for some reason I just could not make myself look away.

Then suddenly her eyes flicked open, staring right at me. She took a deep, noisy breath, and slid quickly back off the rock into the water.

"I'm sorry, I wasn't… I mean…" I started to call after her, but she had submerged and would not be able to hear me. For a moment I could see her outline under the surface then I lost sight of her. She must have been thinking I was a creepy pervert and I scrambled down the rocky groyne onto the sand of the main cove again. I walked briskly back to the car, not looking at the sea.

When I got home, Anna was still curt with me. Toby was sleeping and I gently picked him up and gave him a cuddle. He didn't stir. I put him back again before Anna could come up and tell me off. Though I'd become an accidental Peeping Tom, the mystery beach woman had at least put my mind at rest as to her fate the other day. She must be a strong underwater swimmer, which explained why I hadn't seen her leave before.

Another week passed and I hadn't mentioned this second encounter to anyone. Rob forgot about his jokes. I became preoccupied with work, as we were close to a major breakthrough in our research. Investigating the acoustic properties of materials is a topic that's pretty much guaranteed to put anyone not involved in the field into a deep coma if you try to talk about it, but our last paper had caused a minor stir in the scientific community. If our theories were proved right, our research would have a massive impact on engineering applications from the aerospace industry to bridge building. We were only weeks away from a significant result.

Over time, it became more of a habit for me to sit there upon the rocks after work, as I needed my own space to relieve the mental stresses of work and home life. I would always leave feeling revitalised. Occasionally there would be other people on the beach and sometimes an ice cream van parked at the top of the cliff, but very often it was just me and the birds. I hadn't expected to see the woman any more but one evening, after a long day at work, she appeared again. The sun had dipped to a low angle, and I'd already been relaxing there for twenty minutes or so, eating a sandwich, when I happened to look over at the flat rock and saw her there, stretched out on her front again. I was quite certain she hadn't been there when I arrived and I sat in plain view. I couldn't be accused of voyeurism today. Her face was turned away from me, but this time I could see she wasn't completely naked. She wore some sort of silvery-grey costume on her lower half. With the lateness of the day it still seemed a bad choice of sunbathing time, but maybe she was just taking a rest during a long swim. I tried not to look at her. She has a right to her privacy, I told myself, even out in the open. I finished my sandwich and packed the wrapper into my pocket so as not to pollute the environment. Then I looked over at the flat rock again and the first event that changed my world happened.

The woman had rolled onto her side, still facing away from me. At first I thought she'd drawn her knees up out of the water. Then she straightened out... and I realised there were no knees. There were no legs at all—only a tail. Long, slender, greyish-silver in colour and what I had thought to be clothing was an actual tail. She swished the tip through the water, moving it in a way that would be impossible if it was merely a costume with legs hidden inside. At that moment she raised it to reveal a fin similar to the feet of a seal, but more fishlike. She spread this out then furled it closed, in a way that reminded me of how cats stretch their claws out for a moment when relaxing. Then she lazily rolled onto her back, spread out her arms, and flopped off the rock into the water.

Mermaids don't exist, I told myself. They can't exist. They're not real! And yet... I'd just seen one. And thinking back to the other times I'd encountered her, I hadn't seen her legs, not at all. That was how she could disappear into the sea and why she was so skittish when I'd seen her. My astonishment made me giddy and I put my hands on the rock to steady myself. I racked my brain to think of an explanation other than 'she's a mermaid', but really, there wasn't one—because she was.

I can't remember what happened that evening after I went home. My thoughts were racing and circling around the bizarre revelation I'd had. I wanted to tell people but at the same time, I knew I couldn't. Those who didn't think I was crazy would simply accuse me of having misidentified a seal or other marine creature. I couldn't concentrate at work the next day either.

"You okay, Jon?" asked Rob. "You keep staring off into space looking worried then grinning. Still concerned about the elasticity coefficient in that sample, eh?"

"Hmm? Oh, yes, something like that. Don't worry. It's nothing."

"Well, if you say so." Rob shrugged and turned back to the computer data displays. Meanwhile, unable to fix my mind to my research, I achieved very little that day. As soon as was practical, I drove along to the cove, scurried down the cliff path at an unsafe pace, jogged across the sand, and scrambled, puffing, up the wet rocks to my usual vantage point.

She wasn't there.

So I sat and waited. I should have called Anna to let her know I'd be delayed but I didn't. Instead I leaned back against the rocks to wait and the swish of the water and constant background of bird calls lulled me asleep. I dreamed the anechoic chamber had filled with water and I swam in it, trying to find a pocket of air while the lights grew ever dimmer until I floated in a black void. Then the world I knew came rushing back as my phone rang.

"Jonathan, where the hell are you?" said Anna. I didn't know what to say, so I figured the honest truth was best.

"Ah, I'm... on the beach."

"What? Why? Don't you know what time it is?" I checked my watch—quarter past eight. I groaned.

"Shit. Sorry. I lost track of time. I just came down here to relax for a bit. It's been a stressful day you know—lots of stuff going on. I'm on my way back now. See you soon, okay?"

"You'd better be home soon," muttered my wife and hung up. Of course when I looked over to the rocks, there was only a herring gull standing there. Dispirited and damp with spray, I picked my way down.

Anna barely spoke to me after I got home, initially suspicious I'd been lying about my location, but then convinced by the sand on my clothes and salt crusted on my shoes. After dinner I had a hot bath, for although summer brought some warmth to the day, falling asleep on the shore had left me chilled. I went to say good night to the baby, though he was sound asleep himself.

"Good night, Toby," I whispered, "you wouldn't believe the adventure daddy's been having. Actually, you're probably the only person who would." Toby just sighed in his sleep.

I began to doubt myself a little. I was under considerable pressure... could my mind have played tricks—hallucinations, even? And if it had, how would I know? These thoughts didn't settle the butterflies in my stomach. If anything, they made me keener to return to the beach as soon as possible to verify this possibility. I lay awake again, not disturbed by Toby this time but by the restlessness in my head.

I found the same difficulty concentrating at work again in the morning. My task involved performing calculations using the latest sensor data we had acquired, and I attended to this without my former enthusiasm. It wasn't surprising it was Rob, not I, who spotted the jewel in the numbers.

"Here you go, mate—made you a coffee. You look like you need one... hey, what's that?" Rob frowned and peered at the screen. "Oh, you beauty!" he said, placing the coffee on the desk and dragging a chair over. I hadn't yet seen what he was talking about until he jabbed a finger at the screen.

"Look at that, Jon. The figure is way higher than we predicted based on the standard vibration model." The numbers became clear to me and they meant the theory we had been working on for the last two years was finally proved to be one hundred percent correct. We looked at each other, beaming smiles on both our faces.

"That makes all the sweating in the damned chamber worthwhile, doesn't it?" I said. "Have we got any champagne?"

"Champagne? What's wrong with my coffee?" said Rob, breaking into a laugh. "I think there might be a beer in the fridge though." He rubbed his forehead and sighed.

"Next thing is to get this written up and published."

"It's going to make some waves in engineering circles—you can bet. We might even win that award you're itching to get your hands on," I joked. Rob made no secret of his ambition to win a Nobel Prize one day, which in our field was about as likely as winning an Oscar.

"All right, it's not going to get us a Nobel, but even so—there's the World Tech Awards, the Körber Prize… who knows what fame and glory awaits us!"

We double- and triple-checked the results, sent some e-mails and made some calls, then finished early for the day. I leaned on my car to ring Anna and tell her the news but the call went to the answerphone. Having reached the destination of my professional journey satisfied me greatly, yet still other things left me unsatisfied. The time had come to visit Trelanton Cove again.

Despite the heat of the day in high summer, it surprised me to find the main beach deserted. As I climbed the rocks, I craned my neck to peer over into the little bay beyond, hoping. When the flat stone island came into view I was disappointed not to see the mermaid there. But turning to the little raised bump by the cliff wall that was my customary seat, I paused, for something had been placed there.

It was a circle of twisted plant stems with some small stones and shells woven between them. It looked very like a bracelet and I picked it up. The texture of the stems told me they were seaweed. It must have taken some skill and dexterity to fashion it into such a shape, I thought. Then I realised its creator was watching me. She lay on the beach itself, rather than on the rock, so I had not seen her. I froze briefly when I saw she was looking directly at me, but not fearfully. She smiled warmly, looking relaxed, lying on her side with her tail fin washed by the waves that reached highest on the beach. Holding the bracelet in my hand, I slowly began to descend from the rocks into the mermaid's cove. I had to keep looking where I put my feet so I didn't slip and tumble on the wet stone and each time when I looked back at her again, I expected to find her vanished. But she didn't move, simply remained still and smiling.

My feet touched sand and I walked the few paces over to where she lay then crouched down to her eye level.

"Hello," I said.

"Hello," she replied. There was a pause then I held out the bracelet.

"Um… I found this. Is it yours?" I said. Internally, I scolded myself for such a lame thing to ask a mythical creature. She arched an eyebrow.

"No, it's for you—although I did make it." Her voice sounded like that of a normal young woman. Now I could see her close up and she really was alluring. Her eyes were dark brown, with long, delicate lashes, and her fine-featured face and slender upper body had skin paler than a land-dwelling Caucasian. Her very dark grey hair—almost black—reached to her waist, much of it braided into locks adorned with small shells. Her amazing silvery-grey tail was not scaled, but reminded me rather of the skin of a dolphin. From this distance, I could discern a mottled pattern on it too. She looked about twenty years old by human reckoning and she wore only a thin necklace of a similar design to the bracelet, made from twisted seaweed. She took her latest craftwork from my hand and slipped it over my wrist, where it fit perfectly.

"I've been watching you for a while," she said. "I've seen you come and sit on the rock there, carrying the weight of your thoughts."

"I've seen you a few times too. I thought I scared you away."

"I was cautious at first, yes. Not all who see me are gentle. Often when you were there looking out to sea, I'd be hiding under the spray and waiting. After a while I knew you were not there to hunt me, for you carried no net, no spear, or cage. And you remained even when I was hidden. On many days you looked sad."

"Well, yes, I suppose I wasn't really sad, just, well—"

"You were sad," she interrupted. I fell silent. "But today you're not!" She flashed a radiant smile and motioned for me to sit on the damp sand, which I did, heedless of the consequences.

"My name is Jonathan, by the way. Jonathan Moore. And thank you for the bracelet."

"I am Kerra and I'm glad to meet you, Jonathan. I have rarely spoken to land-men. It's not always safe." She looked up at the kittiwakes flapping to and from the sheer cliff above us, and I realised what gave her the confidence to come ashore here. The birds were a natural early warning system—they always hooted and chattered when I arrived on the rocks and would do so if they saw anything they felt was a threat. Nobody could see us except from the sea or if they came right to the edge of the cliff and leaned over.

"This might sound silly to you, Kerra, but I never knew there were… people like you, until the first time I saw you on the rock there." Kerra cocked her head and looked surprised.

"Really? Did nobody tell you of mermaids?"

"Yes, there are stories about them but most people think they are fiction." I felt a little shamefaced explaining this to the living, breathing creature before me. She looked even more bemused.

"But people see us fairly frequently—sailors out at sea, people watching from the coast—why would they not believe the stories when they see with their own eyes?" I pondered her question for a moment.

"I guess they either think they are mistaken about what they saw or are too worried that nobody will believe them. The sightings of mermaids from sailors in the past were explained as misidentified manatees, seals, and such like." Kerra's increasing astonishment escalated into laughter.

"Do you think I look anything like a seal?" she asked, stretching out on her back on the sand. She certainly did not. In fact, despite her somewhat inhuman lower half, she was one of the most beautiful women I had ever seen—and one with a charming personality as well. I had more questions I wanted to ask her.

"Are there more of your kind around here?" I indicated the Atlantic, looking serene and blue today. She nodded and looked out to the water, raising herself up on her elbows.

"There are, but I must tell you about them another time. I should go before the currents turn. There are things I have to do." She moved snakelike on her tail into the surf. It seemed too soon for her to leave.

"Will I see you again?" I said, feeling a little nervous.

"If you come here tomorrow, you will," said Kerra brightly and with a toss of her head, she made that deep, noisy breath in and out, and plunged below the surface. I felt an instant twinge of loss and an immediate sense of being too far away from her. Strange, I considered, since I really didn't even know my new friend. As I replayed the encounter in my mind, though, my feeling of loss was quickly replaced by the sheer awesomeness of the moment.

I walked back to my car grinning like a fool, not caring about my damp and sandy clothes. It's hard to top the happiness of reaching the successful conclusion of two years of ground-breaking research but conversations with a mermaid will do it every time.

Anna had got home again by the time I arrived and had picked up the message I'd left. She gave me a hug as I came in the door.

"That's such great news, Jon! I bet you're glad you don't have to—ugh, why is your bum all wet?" She jumped back from me. I laughed.

"Oh, it's nothing nasty. I went to the beach again. The sand wasn't quite dry."

"What is it with you and that beach? Who did you go

there with?" Anna shot me a sceptical look.

"Er, I just went on my own," I said, which was technically true. Anna shook her head.

"You're weird, you know. Anyway, are you going to be spending less time at the lab now you're done with the practical testing?"

"A little less, yes. Rob and I need to prepare a paper for publication and do a thorough re-check on all the figures—but lots of that I can do from home. It'll give me more time to help you with looking after Toby."

"I manage perfectly all right looking after him. If you want, I might let you babysit for a day."

"I'm his dad. It's not babysitting! Most mothers would be glad to have their husbands help with baby chores a little more." Anna pulled a sour face.

"Don't call it baby chores. It's important bonding time. The mother is the most important person in a baby's life at his age. You know he needs to feed on demand and I don't want him being given a bottle unless it's absolutely necessary. He'll get sucking confusion and forget how to do it right. You can help with other household tasks while I look after him."

Even with the elation of the day's events, this frustrated me. I wanted to be a good father. I wanted to spend time with Toby and give Anna some space to relax for herself, but she wasn't open to that idea. According to her, I didn't hold him right. I didn't play with him the correct way, or even change his nappy properly. And Anna never seemed in any hurry to educate me, just to tick me off for my faults. She accumulated childcare information from the Organic Babymother's forum on the internet and scoffed at the parenting help books we'd bought in preparation while she was pregnant. I was beginning to worry my son would forget who I was. Anna hadn't noticed the bracelet round my wrist, which I had forgotten until now. I took it off and hid it away in my desk drawer.

When I was done at the lab the following day, I had my fingers crossed Kerra had told the truth and indeed she had. This time she sat on her usual sunbathing rock and on seeing me arrive, she slipped into the water and was on the shore in moments.

"I'm glad you came back," she said. "I enjoyed talking to you yesterday."

"Me too. It was an unusual experience."

"But in a good way." Kerra coiled her tail round behind her much in the way someone sitting sideways on the ground might bend their knees.

"Can I... may I ask a little about how you live? What do you eat and things like that—if you don't mind?" I said.

So she told me of her underwater life. I learned that mermaids lived in communities of between twenty to thirty-five individuals, many of them related to each other. They ate fish, certain types of seaweed, and molluscs such as mussels and clams. Octopus and cuttlefish were a special delicacy and, of course, nothing was cooked. The maids lived in the shallower water as they needed to return to the surface to breathe, though they could hold their breath for forty-five minutes if they had to. The maids farmed food much as we do and needed to tend to their fields of seaweed at certain times, depending on tides and currents, which was why she'd had to leave when she did yesterday. They had their own language but tended to learn the language of the land they lived near, as they heard it spoken often. Kerra had two older sisters, twins Kensa and Tamon, who lived with her, and her younger sister, Zethar, who had migrated somewhere northwards. Her description confused me, as she didn't know our place names or much about the land, but as far as I could tell, Zethar lived somewhere near Cardigan Bay. My estimate of her age was not far wrong, as she was twenty-four years old. Her species had a lifespan similar to ours.

In return, I explained about my life. She found this fascinating, for like most of her kind, her knowledge of 'land-men' extended only to what she could see from the coast and heard talked about by fishermen and holidaymakers. She knew nothing at all of science, and I had difficulty explaining the purpose of my job, as mermaids used no actual machinery. She was comfortable thinking of me as 'someone who helped make tools'. She already understood our family units and childcare and my descriptions of Toby delighted her. She admitted to often playing with children here on holiday—who probably then went back and told their parents they'd met a mermaid and were scolded for lying. Kerra had not tasted cooked food in her life, so I offered her a bit of bacon sandwich I'd packed for lunch but not been hungry enough to eat. She declared the bacon and lettuce delicious but found the bread disgusting.

I'd brought a tarpaulin from the car to sit on, mindful of the state of my jeans, and Kerra wanted to sit on it with me, resulting in it becoming wet anyway and covered with a reasonable amount of sand that had stuck to her body. We talked for a couple of hours until the needs of the tide called her back again and she descended to her home.

The next day we met again, and the day after that, until gradually we were seeing each other most days after I finished work. Slowly we got to know each other and the ways of our respective worlds. We talked about everything and anything, becoming ever more relaxed and comfortable. The ways of the merfolk seemed so much less complicated than human society with its many distractions. I felt a pang of envy when Kerra described the kelp forests, undersea caves, and sandy gardens where she and her clan roamed.

Our acquaintance blossomed into friendship and although at first I denied it to myself, my feelings for her continued to strengthen and grow. We drew the outlines of sea creatures in the sand and compared our race's different names for them.

"What is that?" I asked, after Kerra had doodled

something that bore no resemblance to anything on earth.

"We call that a stensow. You must know them! Wait a moment." She slid over to a small rockpool and after a moment peering into it, grabbed something, which she brought over to me enclosed in her hand.

"A crab?" I said, as she opened her fingers, letting the tiny stensow escape to freedom. "Seriously, Kerra, that's the worst drawing of a crab I've ever seen. You can't blame me for not getting it."

She pouted and made a playful flick of her tail across the drawing, erasing it and not at all by chance showering me with sand grains.

"Oh, you're covered. Let me brush that off," she teased, flapping her fin all over me and depositing even more sand. We giggled like children as we grappled.

I had never known anyone quite so enchanting. No wonder folk stories told of sailors attracted to these maids... I couldn't help myself. And it wasn't just a one-sided feeling; Kerra's smile as she greeted me, the way she folded her fingers between mine as we talked, all told me that she looked forward to my visits as much as I did, for the same reasons.

In August, Anna went to spend a few days with her mother, taking Toby with her. I spent a whole night at the beach with Kerra. The hot, humid air made me clammy and Kerra suggested I might like to join her in her natural environment. I stripped off my clothes and took to the water. We swam together beyond where I'd be happy to go alone in the darkness, knowing she kept me safe. We bobbed offshore, my arms around her waist and her tail supporting my legs, the stars of Pisces, the two fishes, rising in the sky above us. It was a magic time.

"Do you like the water here?" Kerra whispered in my ear, her cheek resting against mine.

"Mmm... it's strangely comforting, even though normally I'm a little nervous when I'm beyond my depth."

Kerra stroked my neck then leaned back, her arms floating outstretched.

"The sea gives life to my kind. Now you're with me, you can sense it yourself. Mermaids are part of the water and it is part of us. It holds us in its arms, you and I."

We returned to the beach and slept, lying against each other. I felt no coldness with her beside me.

I knew I was being disloyal to Anna. I can't deny that. Despite my increasing attraction to Kerra, I had made vows to my wife. She and I had been perfectly happy for the two years we'd been married before Toby came along. We had both wanted children, but I longed for the closeness we'd had before his birth. The love that had radiated from her to me was now directed to our son, and I was trying to warm myself by a distant ember. It had been months since Anna had allowed me in bed with her. She refused to allow me to take care of Toby for more than a couple of hours at a time, with a vehemence bordering on paranoia. Toby himself seemed happy, content, and healthy. His needs were satisfied. Mine were not. What were the needs of the maid I lay next to now?

* * * *

Rob and I finished work on our paper and submitted it for publication in the scientific literature. We could do no more on that particular project and the final professional weight lifted from my mind. But the tension between my commitment to Anna and my desire for Kerra's company tainted the freedom it granted me. We had not kissed or been physically intimate in any other way, but an emotional connection had been made that gained strength every time we met. I was happiest when we were together and I felt an emptiness when we were apart. I could not help the joy that filled me when I was in Kerra's presence, a stark contrast to the frustration and disappointment at my inability to engage in the lives of my wife and my child.

On the first of September, a miserable, grey day with rain dropping like cold tears, I raised a subject with the mermaid that was conspicuous by her deft skirting round all my previous mentions of it.

"So, where *are* all the mermen? I only ever hear you speak of the women in your clan."

Kerra looked a little sad, the rain splashing her gorgeous face. She paused a moment before replying.

"There are no natural mermen, Jon."

"What do you mean?" This confused me. She was a mammal, with all the standard physiological features of the class, for all that she was unusual. There would be no way to reproduce without males.

"Mermen do not come from the sea. They come from the land. They start as land-men like you and they become like me when… when we take them to be with us." She looked down at the beach, seeming discomposed.

I remembered the tales from folklore—mermaids stole sailors from ships and dragged them to the depths or seduced them with their singing. In a flash my perspective shifted as the disturbing truth dawned.

"You take men like me and plunge them into the water to turn them into mermen! What happens to them? Do you take them without consent?" Kerra looked uncomfortable at my accusatory tone, folding her tailfin tight like a closed fan—a sign I had come to learn meant distress or sadness. I tensed, ready for flight, afraid she might suddenly try to snatch me down. Those lithe arms that could catch a fish as it darted past could surely grip hard enough.

"I haven't! Some of us have taken men against their will but I never could. Please don't be frightened of me, Jonathan. Please don't… leave me." Her voice had become small and trembling and she suddenly kicked her tail and leaped right into the water. She slapped her fins down hard against the surface a couple of times, made a crying sound, then shot out to sea at amazing speed, not fully submerged. Soon she sank out of sight.

That evening I pondered Kerra's intentions. Had she been planning to spirit me away to her undersea fields? Anna grumbled that I spent far too much time staring into space these days, little knowing how much churned around in my mind.

I didn't return to the beach for a week. With each day I didn't see her, I missed my friend more and more. Even if she was planning to turn me into a fish or invite her sisters to pick the flesh off my drowned bones, I cared about her. It was an emotion beyond my control. After seven days the need to see her took me back there.

Rain pattered gently over the north coast, making the cliff path muddy and treacherous. Unsurprisingly I was the only human at Trelanton Cove, though not the only person. Kerra flung her arms around me as soon as she could reach me.

"I'm sorry. I'm so sorry," she whispered. "Do you forgive me for scaring you?"

"I wasn't scared, Kerra. Just… surprised, I guess. I've never seen you react that way, you always seem so gentle and calm."

"Let me tell you everything about it then. But please, may I ask a favour first?"

"Yes, of course."

"Will you take me higher onto land? To the top of the cliff? I have longed to see the view from there." She pointed to the path.

"If that is what you want, then yes," I said. With her arm round my shoulders, I picked her up under her back and tail. She weighed little, which made her easy to carry, although going over the rocks and up the path made me worry I'd drop her and cause a fatal injury. I panted with the effort by the time we reached the brow of the cliff. Kerra looked around, entranced.

"The land here goes on so far! I'd never imagined it would look like this," she said. The rain grew heavier and she reached up her arms to let it run down over her, laughing.

"Perhaps we should get in the car? I'm not quite as waterproof as you." She nodded, and I laid the tarpaulin on the back seat, placed her on it then climbed in with her. She marvelled at the car too, having seen them from the outside many times but never having had the opportunity to see the interior.

"I need to explain more about mermen to you," she said, her voice more serious now. "It is true there have been occasions where some of my race have taken men against their will. But it's not our custom in these waters and hasn't been for many generations." She wriggled round to lean her head against my shoulder while she spoke.

"We have only female children born to us. Every baby, for as long as anyone can remember, has been a maid. We love them and cherish them as you do your children, yet when we are grown, we crave the company of males. If we wish to bear children then we need them, as we need water to swim in and air to breathe." She sounded so wistful that I felt terrible for being upset with her.

"When I first watched you, sitting alone on the rock," she said, "I wanted to know more about you. You intrigued me. And I was right in my guess that you are not like other men. You long for fulfillment, for recognition— to be valued for who you are. I think you often feel that, don't you?" I nodded. She was correct, of course.

"You're very perceptive," I said, "I think you know me as well as I know myself sometimes."

"When we had spent a little time together, I wished I could take you as a husband. I'm not ashamed to say it. And as we grew to know each other better, so I wished that even more, but also knew I could never ask you. Because despite all I feel for you, it would not be right. I can't ignore you have commitments in your life and I must respect those, but there are also other reasons of even greater importance."

"What reasons?" I creased my brow, mystified.

"There is a terrible price the land-men pay for life as one of my kind. A land-man will find his legs become a tail. He will find his strength increased and he will not become cold, even in the darkest waters. All these gifts will be his. But his mind will also be lost to him. First, he will begin to lose his memory of life on land and by the time his tail is formed, he will not remember any of it. For three or four years he will be happy among the maids and will give his maidwife many fine baby girls. But then the real price will be paid. He will begin to forget his life as a merman too. He will cease to be able to recognise the maids of the clan and eventually his own maidwife and children. He will become angry and confused, unable to farm the fields or protect us from danger. After a time he will begin to dive deeper and deeper, only just able to return for air. Until the day comes for every merman when he swims to the deepest part of the ocean he can reach and returns to us no more."

Her unsettling description sounded to me like some horrible form of dementia. I imagined the mermen sailing down into the darkness of the abyss, their wives doomed to know this day would come from the moment their husbands entered the water with them.

"Do you remember your own father?" I asked quietly. She shook her head.

"I was only tiny when he left us. Mother was still pregnant with Zethar. Tamon and Kensa have a few vague memories of him, I think." She reached up and touched my face.

"I couldn't do that to you, Jonathan. I couldn't. Your mind is exceptional among your people and you have discovered things that will change your world. I cannot take that from you. To know that all you are will dissolve in the sea is a fate I won't bring upon you."

Her eyes closed as she rested her head on me and I gently stroked her braided hair. A ping from my phone broke the peace. Pulling it from my pocket, I saw a text from Rob had come in.

One gaint leap 4 Rob & Jon!!! Call me wenh u get this!!! I consistently found it amazing that the man was a genius and yet couldn't get his fingers to slow down long enough to spell correctly when he texted.

Eventually, with the daylight fading, I carried Kerra back to the sea. A couple of hours later, back in my warm study, I phoned Rob.

"Hi, I got your text. What's up?"

"Jon, you are never going to believe this!" said Rob excitedly. "You know who I got a call from this afternoon?"

"No. Who?"

"You'll never guess!"

"I'm sure I won't. You'd better tell me, Rob."

"Donald Kahn!"

I paused, unsure who Donald Kahn was and why Rob was so thrilled to hear from him.

"Right... should that name mean something to me?"

"Donald Kahn is the head of materials research at NASA—as in the American space programme!"

"Yes, I know what NASA is." Now the 'giant leap' quote made more sense. "So what did he want?"

"He read our paper. He was well impressed. He wants us to come and work for them over in the USA—can you imagine? We'd get our own lab. We'd get real in-flight testing of our experiments, not just simulations in the chamber. It's gonna be fantastic, mate!"

This bit of news stunned me. It transpired Rob had already said yes to him and rather prematurely assured Kahn that I would also agree to the proposal. I told Rob I couldn't give a definite answer yet.

"What do you mean you want to think about it? It's the deal of a lifetime! Things this exciting don't come along every day," he said, attempting to persuade me.

"Let me chew on it for a day or two. He's not gonna

demand an answer right away, okay? Good night then, Rob."

I considered what this might mean for my little family. Could it be a new start that would bring some love back into my marriage and maybe rekindle what used to be between me and Anna?

* * * *

I gave Anna the news. Her response was instant.

"You're not going to America, Jonathan."

"Well, obviously I wouldn't go without you and Toby. Wouldn't you be happy to move out there? The Ames Research Center is in California. It's sunny all the time, not just a couple of days a year like here in Cornwall."

"I have no desire to live in California, even if it is sunny. Do you want our son to grow up in a country where everyone carries guns? Where they get knifed at school?"

"Don't be silly, Anna. It's not like that. They don't—"

"Absolutely not. That's all I have to say about it. But…"

"What?" I asked. She was not meeting my eyes but clearly still had more to say.

"We have to face the truth, Jon. Things aren't the same as they once were between us. You said you'd be cutting down on work hours but you're still at the lab just as much as ever. And even when you come home your mind is elsewhere. I'm not happy."

"Anna, I do my best. Sometimes work needs more time than I thought it would and I really do want to spend time with you and Toby. I want to be a good father but you really don't give me much of a chance to do that, even when I am here. I do wish I had more free time. Give it a couple of weeks and I'll be done with the new data we're looking at and that'll take the pressure off. I want to work on being a better father to Toby."

But Anna was not mollified.

"No. It's been a problem for too long. When you're here at home, your head's in the clouds, never concentrating on what I have to say. When I went to visit Mum I talked to her about it, and she agreed with me... it could be good for us to separate."

My stomach lurched on hearing this. How had our relationship become that bad?

"Listen," I protested, "you don't need to go that far. Tell me what to do and I'll do it. Let me fix this up! I want Toby in my life. I want us to be a happy family."

"I don't think it will be easy to fix right now. I need space. I'm going to stay with Mum in Donegal, and Toby's coming with me." I felt almost a panic rising at her mention of taking Toby, but I realised if she was to leave then there was no way I could manage to care for him alone. The door that had started to close between father and son from Anna's obsessive childcare was almost shut, and I could think of no way to prevent the final slam.

I stood unmoving as my wife turned and walked away from me, muttering under her breath.

The rain trickled down the window outside, and a rumble of thunder sounded from far away. I sat in my study chair, fingertips pressed to my forehead, trying to deal with the sense of loss I already felt. I no longer cared about the NASA job offer. Since starting work at Mayfield Labs, my research had been my consuming passion—to the detriment of other parts of my life. I knew I had tried in my way to be a good father to Toby but the combination of my long work hours, my personal distraction, and Anna's obsessive parenting had rung a death knell to my marriage and my visions of happy family life. Now all the work and accolades seemed trivial, unimportant to me compared to what I needed as a person, as a human being.

Now my chance at happiness was over. Another slow growl from the sky seemed almost to underline the realisation that my dream of raising children in a loving, happy family unit was gone, likely never to reappear.

Hours passed as I mourned the loss of my life as I knew it. Then slowly, ever so slowly, an alternative plan began to take shape. The failure of my marriage wasn't all my fault. I deserved happiness. And I would have it, even if only for a time…

The sun shone between racing clouds the next morning, with a stiff breeze blowing from the north. Rob had e-mailed me Donald Kahn's contact details with a note urging me to call him and say yes as soon as possible. But I already had a meeting to attend. I drove to the beach, thinking about everything going on in my life and what those things meant to me—Toby, the NASA job, Kerra, Anna—all balanced against each other, all conflicting, pulling me in different directions. I needed to have just one direction. I needed simplicity. I knew what course I must follow. It made me nervous to think about it, but also gave me hope and excitement. Kerra was lounging on her flat rock when I arrived. The autumn water would have numbed my limbs in an instant today and I marvelled at how the chill didn't bother her in the slightest as she swished over to me. I gingerly carried her onto the rocky ridge between the coves, away from the spray.

"I've been thinking about what you were telling me yesterday," I said, "about the mermen." Kerra nodded solemnly.

"I could never force that on you, Jon."

"I know. I trust you. But you did say you wanted me to come with you, didn't you?"

"Yes. My heart wishes for it. To care too much for a land-man I may not have is my crime; it is also my punishment." Her perfect face was calm, accepting this. I placed my hand on hers.

"But you don't have to force it on me. Kerra, I want to go with you."

She looked up, startled. This time the graceful fan of her tail opened wide—hope and happiness.

"I mean it," I continued. "I've thought hard about it and of all the paths I could follow, it's the one I want the most."

"But—your son, your wife! You would leave them?"

"I have come to realise I've already lost them." I gave her a brief summary of the previous evening's events. She listened to the tale then hugged me tightly, murmuring something in her own language I did not understand, though its sentiments of sympathy and consolation were plain. When she looked up at me again, a glint of sunlight sparkled from a tear on her cheek.

"You said I'd forget my land life, isn't that right?" Kerra nodded. I wiped the tear from her face.

"Well, that's what I want. What I need. When my memory goes, so will the pain of losing Toby. And he's too young to remember me."

"But you will lose your understanding of science too. That's an incredible gift, beyond the knowledge of my people. It's like magic to us."

"If I go with you, I won't need it. I don't even know if I want it anymore." Though my work had been my driving force for so many years, it had cost me my family. Now it held no allure in the face of what nature had to offer me.

"Are you sure? Once this happens, it cannot be undone. You will cease to be one of the land-men forever. And you will only live for…" she trailed off, aware that I knew what the rest of my lifespan would be.

I looked out at the sea, shining bright in the sun, and nodded. I had come to terms with the truth that to be with Kerra, to have a second chance to have the love and family I had always wanted for however brief a time, was what I needed now.

She pulled me close, wrapping her tail tightly around my legs, and for the first time put her lips to mine and kissed me. The kiss seemed to go on forever, making me dizzy, giving me a prickly sensation all over. One part of my mind rationally analysed what was happening—Kerra was transferring some sort of chemical or hormone into my body through her kiss. The rest of me didn't care about the how, eager for the result and overwhelmed by the intensely pleasurable experience.

When the kiss came to its end, the mermaid looked exhausted and slumped in a daze on the barnacled stone. I, however, felt unusually clearheaded and carried her down onto the soft sand. After a minute or two she regained her senses.

"I'll be back here for you tomorrow at dawn," she said and let the sea wash her away from me for the last time.

I sat up the rest of the night. I sent an e-mail to Rob and Donald Kahn, apologising for declining the NASA offer. Then I wrote a letter to Anna, apologising for my short-sightedness in sacrificing our happiness to my drive to succeed professionally. I left out the accusations and bitterness I felt at her role in excluding me from Toby's life, as I reasoned it wouldn't make any difference now. After some deliberation, I even told her the truth about Kerra and my decision to try again to find happiness and a family. She would never believe it, but it gave me peace to write it. Before the sky became light I crept into what had once been my bedroom and left the note on her bedside table. I carefully picked up my infant son.

"Goodbye, Toby. Forget me. Your mother will take care of you. I wish... I could be a better father. I do love you." He sighed briefly, but his eyes did not open. Soon I'd be no more than a dream to him. Soon the heartbreak of leaving him would fade for me too.

I already seemed not to feel the cold and I was certain I could hold my breath longer than I'd ever been able to before. Changes were taking place within my body, not yet visible but detectable. I was about to open the door to leave when I remembered something I'd left in my desk drawer. It had to come too.

I left my clothes folded neatly in the car and with only the seaweed bracelet on my wrist, I walked across the smooth sands of Trelanton Cove, leaving my last footprints. The pink dawn glowed behind the cliffs, stars still visible in the western sky. The sea was like a living being, welcoming me into it. I crossed the rocks between the big cove and the small, to the beach where I'd found the start of a new world. I stepped into the foam, feeling it surge around my ankles, and there I waited. Seagulls rode the wind above me and I looked out at the clean horizon. As the sun rose, so did the mermaid from the waves, ready to lead me to the rest of my life. I took her hand and knew all my loneliness would pass away, transformed into joy and contentment beneath the deep Atlantic.

DEEP SECRETS

CHAPTER ONE

The sea breeze ruffled the young man's blond hair as he steadied himself on his board, his mind and body focused and in balance to make a perfect ride to the shore. Out of the corner of his eye, he noticed his friend, Fritz, getting in position to ride the next wave. He smiled, knowing Fritz would not handle it as impressively as he would.

The wave swelled upwards, beginning to break, and he charged down from the lip to a backhand position on the face, difficult with waves as messy as these. But he'd been surfing for years and had the skill to match what the sea could throw at him. He was not going to allow himself to fail, not while Priya was watching from the beach. He'd boasted to her of his prowess with a surfboard, and he intended to make his words ring true. He sped in towards the shore, always just ahead of the sea, and was ready as the wave rolled over and spread itself out to nothing, swishing out right in front of his girlfriend. Priya clapped and cheered.

"Fantastic, Toby! That looked amazing," she said. Toby waded out of the foam and leaned over to kiss her. She broke off from the kiss and pointed out to sea, where Fritz carved his wave.

"Now that's bold of him," Toby said, as Fritz attempted to cut back the way he'd come, along the face. But he didn't turn quite right. Abruptly he tumbled off the board and the wave drilled down on him. Priya screwed her face up and gasped in sympathy. Toby just laughed.

"Oh, he ate it! That's what you get for showing off," he said, watching his friend emerge from the waves and stomp up the beach towards them. As he neared them, he held up the board to show Toby.

"I broke a bloody fin! Can you believe it?" One of the fins on the underside of the board had cracked across, still in one piece but now liable to break entirely.

"You must have hit the bottom then." Toby grimaced, assessing the damage. "Quite a pounding you got there."

"Yeah, it was," said Fritz, not smiling. "I think I clipped that rock there; that's what did it. I preferred the surf over at Sennen, to be honest."

Toby smiled broadly. "Porthleven's not for the faint-hearted. Come on. Let's get a bite to eat. It's not like you'll be doing any more surfing today, is it?" He winked and hoisted his surfboard under one arm, put his other round Priya's waist, and strolled with her towards where they'd parked his car.

Demelza's Cafe gave its customers a fine view out to sea, all in cosy comfort. Though she was off duty, Priya's job as one of their waitresses got her a discount, so the cafe had become the default venue for a post-surf snack. Over scones and coffee, Toby and Fritz talked about their plans for the following day.

"Are you taking the new tagging pole out tomorrow?" asked Fritz.

Toby nodded.

"Yep. It's the first test of it in the field. I'm pretty confident it will work well—if we can find a shark, of course." He looked over at Priya, who wore a slightly worried expression.

"Are they dangerous, these sharks?" she asked. "I

mean, they're big, aren't they? I've never seen one, but from what you told me…"

Fritz chuckled. "Nah. Basking sharks are almost toothless. They just filter plankton out of the water. The worst they could do is swat you with their tail, but they're docile animals."

"Right. And what are the tags for?"

"They have a radio transmitter on them. The sharks are migratory. They turn up all round the British coast, especially here in Cornwall, then they swim away to who knows where." Fritz paused while he reached for his third scone. "By tracking the signals, we can work out where they go. Scientists have been tagging and tracking basking sharks for years, but the data is still sketchy."

"And that's where the Marine Monitoring Service and I come in," said Toby. "This study will get us the best information yet on what these big fish get up to when they're not… well, basking!"

"I see," said Priya, taking a sip of her coffee. "And to think, just a month ago when I met you, you were cataloguing crabs!"

Fritz giggled at this through a mouthful of scone, but Toby wasn't bothered.

"All marine life is important," he said. "What affects one creature affects countless others, and we're only just beginning to understand the sea's ecosystems."

"And I don't understand them at all," joked Fritz.

"That's why you're still an undergraduate student and I have the knowledge of Poseidon himself," said Toby smugly. Now Priya laughed.

"Hey, don't get cocky. You only graduated two years ago," she reminded him.

"Yeah, whatever. Anyone want another coffee?"

The next day brought fine weather, and the sea sparkled as Toby and Fritz readied their small boat, *Hurricane,* in Mullion harbour. The Marine Monitoring

Service had a programme going among fishermen in the area that encouraged them to report basking shark sightings. The gentle giants of the shark family had a habit of floating near the surface and were often spotted. Fishermen who saw them called in the sighting to the MMS, who then sent the location on to Toby. He, in turn, travelled to the area as quickly as possible to try and find the shark. Toby Moore was one of five MMS staff assigned to this task and he covered the south-western end of Cornwall. His assistant, Fritz Chadwick, was not actually employed by the MMS but was getting some practical experience under his belt while studying for his marine biology degree. Though he tended to treat Fritz with cheerful disdain, Toby valued the help, as he could not both apply the tag to the shark's dorsal fin and steer the boat at the same time. What his assistant lacked in surfing skill he made up for with boat handling ability.

The tags themselves were a new type, with a smaller transmitter and an improved applicator at the tip of a long pole, allowing the researcher to tag the shark swiftly and quite painlessly. Toby had been involved in their design process and was eager to put them to the test at last. Some days when he was on tag duty, Toby never received any calls at all. At other times he went to the area but could not find the shark. Eventually, the plan was to persuade the fishermen to carry tagging equipment themselves, but Toby's prototype needed to be trialled first.

When they had loaded the boat, Fritz and Toby sat on the harbour wall and enjoyed the sunshine, unable to do anything further until they were sent a shark alert. Fritz lit a cigarette and watched the people wandering up and down the quayside.

"I guess it's well and truly tourist season, huh?" he said.

"Spoken like a true local. Need I remind you, you're from Surrey?" replied Toby.

Fritz laughed. "Yeah, I can't deny it. I like it here. You were born in Cornwall, weren't you?"

"That's right. Mum's Irish, but my birthplace is just a few miles from here."

"It must have been a great place to grow up, fantastic for children with all the beaches and—"

A bleep from Toby's mobile interrupted Fritz. Toby grabbed it from his pocket and read the message on the screen.

"Shark sighted! And not far from here either, just a couple of miles west. Let's go!"

They leaped into the boat and Fritz started up the engine. In a minute they were coasting out of the little harbour, keeping a close eye on their satellite navigation equipment. The peaceful sea was only disturbed by the very gentlest swell coming in from the wide Atlantic Ocean. They passed several fishing boats, one of which was likely to have radioed in the sighting, and shortly afterwards arrived at the coordinates they'd been given. They both surveyed the sea's surface from the deck, their polarizing sunglasses blocking the reflections coming off the water and allowing them to see below.

"There!" shouted Toby, when he caught the ripple of a fin from the corner of his eye. Fritz edged the boat closer, going slowly so as not to scare the gigantic beast away. It swam in a lazy circle and as they got nearer, they could observe the outline of its body.

"He's got to be at least eight metres long, maybe nine," said Toby. "Impressive... maybe the biggest one I've seen. Okay, just a little to starboard please. Hold this speed... that should do it." He readied the pole, gauging the distance carefully. Something swift darted through the water between the boat and the shark, momentarily distracting Toby. *Probably a seal.* They were common in these waters, though he'd never seen one come this close to a basking shark before. He returned his attention to the task in hand, but then Fritz called out from the wheelhouse.

"Toby, be careful. There's someone swimming out here!"

"No, it's a seal. I just saw it go past. Ignore it."

"It's not. It's a woman. I just watched her head pop up from under the water. She's probably a diver, checking out the shark."

"Well, where is she now?" asked Toby, glancing around. He didn't want her to be injured by the boat's propeller. Unable to see any sign of the diver, he readied the tagging pole again, only to see the shark rapidly sinking into the depths—out of sight and definitely out of reach.

"Damn! We lost him."

Fritz came out on deck and peered over the side, just in time to see the last glimpse of the disappearing shark.

"Aww, no! That's bad luck. Maybe he'll come up again in a minute... want to stay out here a while, in case?" he said.

"Sure. We could get lucky. Sometimes they... what was that?" Toby turned to the stern as he heard the noise of something bumping against the hull. Fritz walked to the end of the boat and looked down, expecting to see the shark returning. Instead he jolted back as a hand reached up and grabbed the guard rail of the boat. The woman he'd seen in the water... it had to be her. Recovering his composure, he returned to the side. Toby joined him. Perhaps the swimmer had been hit by the boat and injured, in which case they needed to get her out of the water as soon as possible. The hand was joined by another then a girl's face rose above the rail, framed by a mass of long, blonde hair. She looked to be in her late teens, and her face looked calm, not in pain.

"Are you okay? Did we hit you?" asked Fritz. She didn't answer but merely smiled then fixed her gaze on Toby. Something didn't seem right about her. They were a couple of miles out from shore. She wasn't wearing a wetsuit or goggles and had no snorkel or air tanks. With a sudden pull of her arms she raised herself farther from the water, her whole upper body now visible.

"Oh… okay…" said Fritz, surprised to see her torso was unclothed. But the two men had barely registered this before she pulled herself up even farther, then over the railing into their boat, surprising them even more.

Fritz gaped, speechless, and Toby let out a swear word he reserved for the most extreme occasions. The girl possessed no legs, but a tail—grey, shiny, and muscular, on which she slithered across the wooden planks towards Toby.

The young man stumbled back as she advanced, tripping over his backpack, which lay on the deck. She came closer and he scrambled to stand, but could not. And then the creature spoke.

"Toby… you *are* Toby? I've been looking for you."

"No!" he screamed. "Get away! Leave me alone!" The apparition made no move, just remained there, her face calm and almost smiling. Realising he still held the tagging pole, Toby brandished it like a spear.

"Stay back! Get off my boat!" he yelled, and swung the pole. The creature gasped, her green eyes widening with surprise and pain as it struck her on the side of her tail. She twisted around and in a flash, she leaped off the port side of the boat and into the water.

For a minute, neither Toby nor Fritz could speak or move, though they were both thinking the same thing. Fritz eventually broke the silence.

"Uh… mermaid?"

"Yes. Mermaid," replied the dazed Toby. Fritz then began to laugh, but Toby didn't find anything funny. Something from his past had come rushing back to him, something he had thought to be ravings from the disturbed mind of a man he never knew.

As a marine biologist, Toby considered the concept of mermaids to be ridiculous. Nothing he'd seen in the sea supported evidence of their existence. Once you began entertaining the idea of mermaids, you might as well sign up for belief in pixies, werewolves, and the Tooth

Fairy. He could not—would not—allow himself to believe what he'd just seen.

"Oh man, did you see her face? So beautiful!" said Fritz. "This is the discovery of the decade—of the century! Damned shame we didn't get a photo, and why did you go and scare her off?"

"It knew my name. How?"

"I don't know. She could probably hear us talking before she climbed up into the boat. What does it matter?"

"It said it had been looking for me. Didn't you hear? Hunting me!" Toby flung down the pole he was still clutching and stood at the rail, staring into the blue water. There was no trace of the mermaid. Like the basking shark, she was gone. Toby didn't want her to reappear.

"Let's get back on land," he said.

* * * *

After arriving back at Mullion, they secured the boat and went to have lunch in the pub. Fritz couldn't stop talking about the encounter but Toby remained taciturn. He had tried hard to think of an alternative explanation but reluctantly admitted that the obvious one was the truth.

"If there's one, there have to be others, right?" said Fritz, in between bites of steak pie.

"Not necessarily. That's not a logical conclusion."

"Yes, it is. There's no animal on earth that doesn't have others of its species—unless they've been hunted to the brink of extinction."

"Maybe the others were then. That's why you never see them. Or maybe it's not a true species but some sort of mutated human. In fact, that's much more likely."

Fritz shook his head and took a gulp of cold lager before replying.

"Nah, she was gorgeous. And that was a proper tail, not just fused together legs or something. Did you see the fins at the end? Similar to the flukes of a porpoise but with a bit more structure—maybe with bones in it like seal's feet." He grinned excitedly, unable to understand why Toby was so moody about having met a mermaid. He didn't know the event had awoken hidden memories in Toby's head—memories that made the young man feel uneasy and quickened his pulse. Memories that gave him reason to think of mermaids not as beautiful creatures, but as monsters to be hated and feared.

* * * *

Later that night, Toby could not sleep. He was still restless. Despite being safe on land, lying alone in his flat made him uncomfortable, as if something was hiding in the shadows—unearthly presences lurking and watching him. He picked up his phone and called Priya.

"Toby… what time is it?" she answered, her voice slow with sleep. "Are you all right? It's two o'clock in the morning. What's the matter?"

"Can I… can I come over, please? It's nothing bad. I just don't want to be on my own right now."

"Of course, sweetie. No problem. I'll probably be asleep though."

"That's okay. You can sleep. I'm not gonna work tomorrow, and I know you are. I'll be there in half an hour, okay?"

Toby drove fast to Priya's house in Camborne, seeing very few other cars at such a late hour. She was up and waiting when he arrived and welcomed him with a warm hug. Too drowsy to quiz Toby as to what had perturbed him, she took him up to her bedroom and snuggled against him. Within two minutes, she fell asleep again, and although it took a little longer for Toby to drift into dreams, he managed to do so now he was comforted by Priya's loving presence.

Toby awoke later in the morning to find she had left for work without waking him, and her cat had claimed the warm spot she'd left in the bed. He shoved the purring beast off onto the floor and sat up, stretching his limbs. The rest had calmed his mind a little and he didn't feel as shaken as the day before, but there were things he had to think about and someone he needed to talk to. He thumbed his phone to Fritz's mobile number and called him.

"Hi Tobe. What's up?"

"I'm not going to be able to cover shark call duty this morning. Will you be okay on your own? I know it's not ideal, but there's something I have to do."

"You're afraid to go out there, aren't you?"

"No, Fritz, I am not. It's family stuff… If you aren't happy covering for a while, I'll ring MMS and let them know." Toby was not in the mood to tolerate Fritz's idea of humour.

"I'll be fine. No sweat. Leave it to me."

CHAPTER TWO

Toby showered at Priya's house and texted to thank her for letting him disturb her sleep, promising to make it up to her later. After ensuring he'd locked the house, he went for a short walk to get some fresh air before returning to his car and taking a drive to Redruth—to the family home where he had been born and where his mother still lived.

Anna Moore answered the door with surprise and delight to see her son. He was an infrequent visitor, despite living relatively close.

"Oh, how wonderful to see you, Toby darling! You're looking well. Would you like to stay for lunch?"

"That would be lovely, if you don't mind, Mum," he said. Like most young men, Toby considered his mother's cooking to be a 'must have' treat. Anna ushered him in and made them both coffee.

"I'm sorry I didn't call first," he said, taking the steaming cup.

"Oh, don't be silly. You know you are always welcome, and if I'm out, you know where the spare key lives."

They made idle chitchat for a while. Anna asked him about Priya, as she hadn't seen her son in person since the two of them got together. Then Toby brought the conversation round to the real reason he'd come.

"Mum… can I ask you some things about Dad?"

Anna's eyes widened, which showed Toby she was caught off guard for a moment. She rarely spoke about his father—to him or anyone else. But then her surprise changed to a look of resolve.

"Yes, of course darling. What would you like to know?"

"Well… I know that when he disappeared, he left a note. Didn't he? Can you remember exactly what it said—or do you still have it?"

Anna looked down at the floor for a moment and sighed.

"Yes, he did leave a note, and no, I don't have it any more. The police borrowed it and I told them I didn't want it back. I remember what it said, though. I *have* told you before."

"I know you have, but that was a few years ago. Please, could you remind me again?" he said gently, aware of the pain the conversation was awakening.

"You were under a year old. We'd had a bit of a difficult patch after you were born. Dad's work was taking up much of his time then when he came home, he always seemed to have his head elsewhere—not listening when I talked to him, that sort of thing." She took a sip of her coffee then continued.

"A day or two before he left, we'd had… not really an argument, but I'd told him I wasn't happy and things needed to change. I was considering taking you and moving back to Grandma's house in Donegal. I think that must have been what pushed him to do what he did. Anyway, one day shortly after that, I woke up to find he wasn't in the house. I assumed he'd gone in to work early for some reason, but then I found the note by my bed. I couldn't believe what I was reading. It said that he was sorry things weren't working between us, but he had…" Anna paused, clearly stressed by re-living the memory.

Toby held her hand and she composed herself, resuming the tale.

"He said he had met a mermaid, of all things. He'd met this mermaid and was going off to be with her and live under the sea, goodbye, and to please look after Toby."

Toby heard the long-buried anger now tinge her demeanour.

"I mean, can you imagine anything more ridiculous? Obviously there was some sort of psychological problem that had been going on underneath, perhaps that's why he'd been so odd before he left. I called his work but he wasn't there, and then I called the police. They went to Trelanton Cove, which is where he claimed he'd met her, and found the car with all his clothes inside. And that is all anyone knows. We never saw Jonathan Moore again. The police said it was quite likely he'd just walked into the sea and drowned."

"I'm sorry, Mum. I know you don't like to talk about it, but I really needed to hear it again. It's been… very much on my mind recently." His mother smiled and hugged him.

"It's only natural, Toby. You never knew your father. He wasn't very capable when it came to looking after you as a baby. I don't know if he'd have been much of a good dad when you were older either. But you know I love you very much, don't you?"

"Of course," he replied. But Toby's thoughts were in turmoil. *If mermaids are real, then Dad's note could have been telling the truth.*

But he couldn't tell his mother what happened yesterday. For twenty-three years she'd believed her husband had drowned himself after a bout of mental illness. Best not to undo that belief with an even more frightening possibility. If his father had really cared about his wife and child, then he would never have left them. A knot of resentment tightened inside Toby, both against his father and the abomination that had taken him from his family.

What had the mermaid done with his father? Eaten him? Drowned him for the fun of it?

They ate lunch and Toby stayed a couple of hours longer before departing. He switched his phone on and messaged Priya, suggesting going for dinner tomorrow, and found a text Fritz had sent just before lunchtime.

I checked the tag pole. There's no dart on it. We tagged her! We can find her again!

Toby was so startled he had to read the message again to be sure. He had thought he'd just hit the mermaid with the side of the pole, but if Fritz was right, the tag had become attached to the flesh of her tail. In his alarmed state, Toby hadn't thought to even check the pole after using it to fend her off. A flush of devious excitement coursed through him, fuelled by a sense of revenge. If this creature had taken his father from him, then maybe they now had a chance to capture it. The radio emitting tag could be located to within a few metres by his receiving equipment.

"We know where you are!" he muttered to himself.

* * * *

Sunshine once again beat down on the tourists taking snaps of Mullion's quaint harbour and on the two men preparing *Hurricane* for her next outing.

"Are you sure, Toby? You really want to try and get her out of the water?" Fritz had been all for trying to track the mermaid down to talk to her, but Toby's ambitious plan was obviously more than he'd been expecting.

"Yes. And then we take it back to land, and we… study it. I've got the use of one of the MMS depots a couple of miles down the road from here. There's a large-size tank in it, easily big enough to put it in."

"It's nice you've changed your attitude at least. Yesterday you seemed almost afraid of her."

"I have my reasons to think that. Don't forget, we

know next to nothing about this creature. It's undoubtedly as strong as a human. It could be aggressive and predatory. We *should* be afraid of it, because it's sensible to be cautious. Don't let the appearance of a beautiful girl fool you. Remember how the angler fish lures its prey with an attractive, glowing light."

"Yeah, I suppose. Anyway, she could be harmless, but it looks like you've already made your mind up about her. What gives? There's something you're not telling me." Fritz narrowed his eyes suspiciously. Toby hesitated for a moment then decided to come clean.

"My father disappeared when I was just a baby," he said. "Everyone always believed he drowned or committed suicide or something. They never found a body. But he left a note, claiming he was running away with a mermaid."

"You are bloody kidding me, right?" Fritz's mouth hung open.

Toby shook his head. "I'm afraid not. Nobody—not me, not Mum—ever guessed the letter was anything more than the ramblings of a man who went off the rails. Then yesterday everything changed. I realised it could be true. And I want to know what happened to Dad."

"No shit. I see where you're coming from." Fritz looked thoughtful. "Dangerous indeed, if she can lure a man to his doom. I'm sorry about your father, Toby. It must have been hard for your family."

"I don't remember it myself. I never really felt I missed out as a kid, but I didn't know any different. Mum hardly ever talked about him. From what she's said over the years, he was a jerk anyway."

Fritz fell silent, not knowing what to say. Toby carried on loading equipment into the boat—the VHF tracking receiver first, then a large net and several coils of thin rope. He didn't have a definite plan for exactly how to trap the mermaid, but was hoping she would try to come on board the boat again. This time, they'd be ready.

Hurricane motored slowly out of the harbour under

Fritz's steerage, while Toby studied the tracking receiver's screen intently. A dot, pulsing green, indicated they were picking up a signal from the tag, though the exact direction was not clear yet. As the boat pushed on through the gentle waves and moved further from land, the radius of the dot increased to a circle as the signal improved. Toby determined the rough direction of the trace and called to Fritz to head eastwards. The signal continued to become clearer and stronger, enabling them to track with ever increasing accuracy. The mermaid could not be far away.

After half an hour of travel, Toby shouted to Fritz to cut the engine.

"We're very near… yes, I can see the signal direction changing, even though we're not moving now," he said.

"She must be swimming past us then," said Fritz, as he emerged from the wheelhouse and came to Toby's side. He peered down at the screen with its digital directional indicator.

"If I read this right, our target is about twenty metres away and moving across our bow southwards," said Toby. "Hold on. It's coming back the other way."

"I see her!" Fritz jumped up, shading his eyes then fumbling for his sunglasses. "Over there!"

Toby followed his pointing finger and saw a head above the surface, facing them. Then with barely a ripple, it vanished. Immediately the two men looked down at the tracking screen. Toby made a fist and punched the air.

"Yes! Coming closer. Fifteen metres… ten…"

Then the beautiful face rose above the water and looked straight up at them, almost close enough for them to reach out and touch her. Her expression was serene, yet cautious, and her shimmering blonde hair hung well below the water line, its floating mass concealing her body.

"Would you like to come up on the boat again? We're sorry about, er, what happened last time," were Fritz's nervous words. The maid said nothing at first, but twisted her body in the water to expose the side of her tail above the surface. The tag was plainly visible, embedded in the silver-grey skin. She would not have been able to remove it without causing herself considerable pain.

"Why would you attack me?" she said. "I came in trust to you."

A chill ran through Toby's heart as she spoke. But he would not allow fear to block his goal of getting what he had come for.

"I am sorry. It wasn't intentional. Will you come back aboard the boat?" he coaxed, trying to sound welcoming and friendly. The mermaid flicked her tailfin and swam even closer.

There was a moment of silence while she considered, then her arms reached up to haul her body aboard. She coiled her tail for support and held her slender torso upright, water dripping from her waist-length hair to form a little puddle around her.

"I just wanted to talk to you." Her voice carried a hurt tone.

"Er… I'm Fritz, by the way," said the student, grinning at their visitor. She smiled in return but addressed Toby when she spoke again.

"Toby… I know you don't know me, but I hope… what?"

From the corner of her eye, she had caught a glimpse of Fritz reaching for the net. With amazing speed, she rounded on him, hissing.

"You would trap me! Why?" Panicking, Fritz's only response was to try and throw the net over her. She became tangled in it, but her strong tail lashed out at Fritz and knocked him to the deck. The impact made him release his hold on the net and the mermaid pulled herself as quickly as she could to the side of the boat. She flipped over the edge, dragging the net with her. Toby leapt to the guard rail, snatching up a boat hook to try and snare the mesh. The mermaid had not submerged or swum beyond reach, encumbered by the net.

He seized his chance and swung the boat hook to try and catch hold, just as she bucked up out of the water. The pole caught her with an almighty whack, right on her waist. The maid cried out in pain and writhed in the webbing, finally beginning to struggle free. But Toby had managed to snare a link and dragged it back towards him before she could get out of it.

"Fritz, rope! Hold the pole for me." As fast as he could, Toby made a loop in the rope and leaned down to slip it over the flapping tail flukes. Tightening it so she could not get away, he wrapped the other end around a stanchion.

"Got her," said Fritz, laying the boat hook down. The mermaid's futile wriggles slowed and weakened as she found herself unable to escape from her undignified predicament, tail fin up in the air and head downwards under the water. Fritz and Toby began to haul her in, causing her to squeal in pain again as she banged her already sore side against the gunwale. Once in the boat, she continued to try and scramble off, but she was exhausted. Every movement was clearly harder than the last. Out of water's supporting embrace, her own body weight counted against her. She took a rasping breath and ceased moving.

"Great. We've killed her," said Fritz mournfully. "The only living mermaid ever caught is now the only dead mermaid ever caught."

Toby knelt beside the still body stretched across the wet deck. Gingerly he touched her wrist, surprised to discover her skin felt exactly like that of a normal human. He held his finger there for a few seconds.

"No. It still has a pulse." He stood up, grim satisfaction making a wry smile on his face. "Let's get back to the big tank, shall we?"

* * * *

A single fixture hung from the ceiling and illuminated the large Perspex tank, casting blue-green ripples of light across the bare floor around it. Their captive floated there, still unconscious. Toby had tethered her in the water so she stayed in a slightly head-up position, to keep her nostrils above the surface. He wasn't certain, but he suspected this creature breathed air rather than having gills somewhere. He and Fritz stood watching her, figuring out what to do next.

"I reckon we should write up a complete description of her. That's what they do when new species are discovered, isn't it? Measure them and weigh them and stuff," suggested Fritz. He positively bounced with excitement and had forgotten about Toby's family history already.

"Yes, that's a good idea." Toby paced round the tank and sighed. "Come on, wake up!" he said to the mermaid, who remained oblivious to all around her. He was desperate to interrogate her, to ask what she had done to his father, and why she was now coming after him. He stared at her serene face, considering the irony of such a lovely countenance belonging to so dangerous a predator—for she truly was perfect in appearance—her pale skin unblemished, except for a darkening bruised area at her waist and thin green lines curling across her belly and up over her chest and back. Her light grey tail had a slight silvery sheen to it and was unscaled. Her fine hair swayed slowly in the tank's currents like fibrous waterweed.

"I'm a bit disappointed she's not wearing one of those shell bras. You know, like they're supposed to?" said Fritz, snapping Toby out of his reverie.

"Don't be stupid. This isn't something out of Hans Christian Andersen. It doesn't sing and frolic with lobsters and dolphins."

"I was joking. Why do you have to be so serious, Tobe?"

"Because this *is* serious! Look what we have here! As

far as we know, we've caught something the scientific world has never seen!"

"True. Do you think we should tell Abbie?" Professor Abigail Lindridge was in charge of Fritz's degree course, and the poor lad was desperate to impress her—for both academic and personal reasons. Toby secretly thought Fritz's interest in his tutor bordered on the obsessive.

"No. Besides your plain intent to use it as a means of getting into Abbie Lindridge's knickers, we can't tell anyone about this just yet. Not until we're ready. Nobody's going to steal our thunder."

* * * *

They spent the rest of the afternoon documenting their catch. They measured her tail length, weight, and every other dimension of her. They took photographs from every angle. With care, they removed the tag with which they had tracked her down. Throughout it all, the mermaid remained unconscious, laid out on a wide bench. When they were done, they made sure she was secure in the tank before Fritz left. Toby wanted to stay overnight on guard, eager to be there if she should wake.

Night fell, and Toby was in the process of drafting a write-up of their data when his phone rang.

"Toby, where are you?" said an aggrieved Priya. "We were meant to be going out to eat this evening. Did you forget?"

"Uh, yes. I'm so sorry Priya!" Toby smacked his forehead as he remembered their date. "I've been so caught up in work today... I'm still doing work stuff right now in fact. Can we make it tomorrow?"

"I guess so... are you all right? I'm not trying to intrude but you seemed really upset the other night when you phoned. You know you can talk to me about it, don't you? It's... it's not something I've done that's the problem, is it?"

"No, Priya. It's not you at all. I was shaken up a bit by a

sea creature we found. It was a little scary. The sort of thing to give you nightmares. Anyway, we've got it in a tank now to study it." Toby didn't want to lie to his girlfriend but at the same time, couldn't tell her the strange truth.

"Ah, I see," she said, sounding a little brighter, "and you're still working on it now?"

"That's right. I'm pretty sure it's a new species."

"Wow! Do you get to name it? The moorefish perhaps?"

Toby chuckled at her suggestion. "I don't know, sweetheart. We'll see."

Does it have a name it calls itself?

Toby pondered that idea long after he'd hung up the phone.

CHAPTER THREE

The next morning Fritz arrived to find the warehouse door unlocked and Toby still at his desk, his tousled blond head resting on it uncomfortably as he dozed. He jerked awake as Fritz entered.

"Bloody hell, Toby. You were here all night? I've got a z-bed you can borrow if you're going to bunk in here."

Toby stretched and yawned, getting up and shaking his leg, which was suffering pins and needles. Fritz walked over to the tank, gazing at the mermaid with admiration.

"And how's our goddess of the sea this morning?" he said, tapping on the Perspex.

"It's not a goddess, it's…"

"Yeah, I was joking again!" grumbled Fritz. "Lighten up, will you?"

Toby sighed and paced closer to examine the mermaid. The bruised area on her torso had spread and become an angry, dark colour. He wished he hadn't hit her quite so hard with the boat hook. For a moment, a twinge of pity for the creature softened his thoughts, but it quickly passed when he looked back up at her face—her eyes were open, looking dozily about her.

Toby grabbed a stepladder and placed it next to the

tank. He climbed up so he could look down into the tank and talk to the mermaid.

"Can you hear me?" he said. She continued staring into space, not responding. He repeated himself a little louder, and this time she turned her head to look at him.

"It's me. Toby Moore," he continued. "You came to talk to me. What do you want with me?"

She took a deep breath of air, wincing and trying to place a hand to her injured abdomen but discovering her wrists were tied securely.

"Toby…" she said, her voice weak and drowsy. She swished her tail slowly then her eyes closed again.

"Hello? Can you still hear me? Hello? Ah, damn it." Toby descended the ladder.

"Well, I suppose it's good she's still alive at all," said Fritz encouragingly. "We may get more out of her later. And it occurs to me she hasn't had anything to eat since yesterday. She might be very hungry."

"That's a good point. We should feed her," Toby nodded. "I'll go and find something… what do you think she eats?"

"Aha! You know what you just did?" exclaimed Fritz. "You just called her 'she'—not 'it', like you have been!"

Toby rolled his eyes. "That's hardly relevant. I refer to Priya's cat as 'she'. It doesn't mean she's not an animal. And we know she's a female."

"Yes, she's got"—Fritz mimed a bra shape with his hands— "and we found her, um—"

"Anyhow, I'm off to find food," Toby interrupted. "Keep an eye on her in case she wakes again, okay?"

Squinting in the summer morning sunlight as he left the warehouse, Toby realised he had no idea what mermaids ate. The possibility of human flesh had crossed his mind already, but he hadn't thought past that. Then he remembered their physical examination of her from the day before. Her teeth were like those of a human, with canines for tearing and molars for grinding. The conclusion must be that like her land-living counterparts, she was omnivorous. A short walk from the waterside warehouse took him to a local fishmonger, who supplied him with some fresh skate and mackerel. The thought of a delicious fish to eat made him realise he'd had neither breakfast nor supper the night before and his hunger was catching up with him also. As soon as he'd got the fish back, he would see about feeding himself, and Fritz could sort out the feeding arrangements for the maid.

When he arrived at the warehouse, Fritz was lounging in a chair by the side of the tank, reading a book.

"Nothing to report, I'm afraid," he said.

"Hmm, well. I didn't think there would be. Listen, I need to get a bite to eat. Can you cut these up for her in case she feels like eating?" Toby handed over the bag of fish.

"Sure thing. Do you think I should cook them?"

Toby pulled a face. "Let me see... does she have an electric or gas powered stove in her underwater kitchen? Would she like them rare or well done?"

"All right. No need to be so sarcastic." Fritz was sullen. "I'll dangle them in front of her and see if she bites."

"Right, okay. Do you want me to bring you back anything?"

"No, I ate before I came out. And I can always eat the mermaid's leftovers, if I get peckish."

* * * *

Toby sought out a nearby fast food outlet and treated himself to a less than healthy meal. Having not eaten in so long left him heedless of what he ate, as long as it filled his stomach and provided energy. He kept thinking about what to do now they had the mermaid under their control. If she regained consciousness and could be made to talk then he would interrogate her, but what then? Release her into the sea? No. All other options would leave him better off. Scientific acclaim for discovery of a new species—if indeed she was—went without saying. He would also be guaranteed considerable sums of money from publicity and exclusive access, maybe to see her exhibited. But then people would challenge his right to keep her captive, as if she had the same rights as a human. But she was not human, for all her top half might appear so. She was an animal, no different from any other non-human species.

But if she died without giving him a chance to speak to her, he could still profit in both those ways. Her body could be preserved and displayed, with no attendant fuss about her right to live free.

In fact, the more he thought about it, the more it seemed the simplest long-term plan was for her life to end at a convenient moment in the not too distant future, once she had yielded what secrets she had to tell. Toby's compassionate heart resisted, appalled at himself for finding his thoughts straying along those lines, but his logical side was winning the battle.

* * * *

When he came back to the warehouse just before noon, he didn't like what he saw.

"What the hell do you think you're doing?" he snarled at Fritz. The student wore only swimming trunks and was sitting in the tank beside the mermaid.

"I figured it was the easiest way to feed her. Otherwise I have to reach over from the top all the time," Fritz explained.

"Did she eat anything?"

"As a matter of fact, yes, she did—some of the mackerel. I waved it under her nose and she came to a bit. Didn't say anything but took a couple of bites, then passed out again. I thought I'd better stay in with—"

"Bloody hell, Fritz!" Toby interrupted. "You've untied her hands! Are you insane?"

Fritz looked sheepish, and Toby scowled up at him, waiting for an explanation.

"I thought she might be uncomfortable. If she does wake up, she's not going to like being tied up, is she? Unless she turns out to be into that sort of thing…" He trailed off, his humour failing to wipe the frown from Toby's face.

"Do I have to put a big sign up on the tank saying she's dangerous? Good grief, have you forgotten how strong she was when we were trying to catch her? She knocked you down with a single strike of her tail."

"She was terrified. We've always been the aggressive ones to her. You stuck her with the tag then we netted her and roped her up. I thought being nice for a change wouldn't be so bad." Fritz climbed out of the tank and down the stepladder at the side.

"She could probably crawl out, numbskull! Or drown you, which might teach you a lesson."

Fritz glared at him.

"I don't know why I work with you anymore, Toby," he said, as he towelled himself dry. "You're always so… so smug and condescending about everything! Okay, so I don't know as much as you about marine biology, and I'm trying to get some experience. I know you didn't have to take me on, but why are you so mean to me all the time? I thought we were friends!"

"We are friends, Fritz. It's just that this is a situation we have to be very careful with."

"Ever since we found her, you've got worse. I know you've had some shocks to deal with but don't take it out on me." Fritz finished pulling on his clothes and flung the towel down on a chair.

"Fritz, I'm not taking it out on you—at least not intentionally. I'm sorry if you're finding me difficult to work with right now, but you must appreciate we're trying to handle something unprecedented. And it's just you and me."

"I know you want fame and glory from this, but why does it have to be only the two of us?" countered Fritz. "I say we should contact Abbie and get help from the university—or even your chums in the MMS. We have to go public sometime; this secret can't stay in the warehouse forever."

"No." Toby was emphatic. "I have a plan for how to proceed."

"Are you gonna clue me in, then?"

"You don't need to know right now. I think—"

"Oh, there you go again," spat Fritz. "I should know my place and not expect to be privy to the grand scheme!" He shook his head and stalked out of the door, slamming it behind him.

* * * *

Toby remained alone in the warehouse for the rest of the day. He texted Fritz to try and make peace but his messages were not answered. Toby himself ignored a couple of incoming shark reports, too wrapped up in his own world now.

At about six in the evening, a splash from the tank brought Toby to alertness. He jumped up from the desk where he had been writing up notes and bolted over to see. He'd re-tied the mermaid's hands, and now she was struggling feebly against her bonds. Toby's heart began to beat faster—perhaps she would be ready to talk. Scooping up some mackerel in case she was hungry again, he ascended the stepladder and leaned over the water. The mermaid's eyes were open and she looked up at him with an expression of such sorrow that for a moment, Toby felt an impulse to untie her and cast her back into the sea. But he got hold of himself, remembering she was undoubtedly a creature of guile and cunning, likely to play on his sympathy to get what she wanted. Well, Fritz might have been fooled, but not him. He held out the mackerel.

"Are you hungry?"

The mermaid nodded and opened her mouth. With great caution, in case she would bite his finger off, Toby placed the morsel of fish between her lips. She chewed it and swallowed, then opened her mouth for more.

"You can have more," said Toby, "but you must talk to me first."

She tried to speak but her voice was a hoarse whisper, and it was obviously an effort for her. He leaned closer in order to hear.

"I will... I must... talk to you." Her eyes closed and her head rested back against the side of the tank, her breathing fast and shallow. The darkened patch on the side of her body was no better. In fact, Toby could see the mark had continued to spread and deepen in colour.

"Tell me something. Did you take Jonathan Moore? Did you take my father under the sea?" Toby's question evidently hit home, for the maid's eyes widened and she strained forward.

"Your father.... father..." she croaked, then slumped back against the side again. Toby's fingers clenched against the rim of the tank.

"Tell me! Did you take him from Trelanton Cove?"

"Your father... came... he came there." Her voice dwindled from the effort. "His... last steps... were there."

His last steps. What did she mean? Had she killed him after all? But he could ask no further questions, for his captive had passed into unconsciousness once again. Toby cautiously reached into the tank and put his hand on her abdomen, applying gentle pressure to the bruised area. She did not wince or twitch. She would not be capable of answering any more questions for a while yet. He locked up the warehouse and strolled to his car, warm in the early evening sunshine.

* * * *

"So come on. Tell me about the moorefish" said Priya, spearing a potato on her fork. To make amends for forgetting their date the day before, Jonathan had taken her out to her favourite restaurant. Getting away from the strangeness of the last couple of days and stepping back into normal life for a while was a relief.

"It's not technically a fish, as such," he said. Priya waited for him to say more but he didn't add any details.

"What is it then? A mollusc?" she asked.

"It's a mammal, as far as we can tell."

"Oh, like a dolphin or seal, right? Cute!"

"Hmm, not quite like that. Fritz thinks it's cute, but…" He trailed off, deciding which way to go with this. Much as he wanted to conceal his find from the world and sort out his personal quest with no complications, he wanted to be honest with her.

"It's a mermaid," he said.

She blinked at him, her eyebrows raised.

"Very funny. What is it *really*?"

"I'm not making this up. We caught a mermaid and we have her in a tank in the MMS warehouse."

Priya burst into laughter, not believing a word. Toby didn't know how to make his tale sound more convincing—but he didn't have to.

"I get it," his girlfriend said. "Because it's a new species, you're not allowed to say anything about it to anyone, right? Don't worry, I won't press you. A mermaid indeed! You're so funny! I'll find out when it gets announced to the world, I suppose."

"Ah, yes. I was kidding with you of course." The best policy now was just to go along with this idea rather than make himself look like a nutcase.

"You know," she said, "when I was a little girl, we were on holiday in Wales. We had one sunny day out of the whole week and we went to the beach. I was playing with my brother round the rockpools and I looked into the sea, and I was sure—just for a moment—that I saw a mermaid in the waves. Of course it must have been somebody swimming—or a penguin or something. But at the time, I really believed it."

"They don't have penguins in Wales, Priya."

"Oh, of course not. You know what I mean, silly." She giggled and the conversation turned to other topics for the rest of the meal.

After dinner, Toby took Priya home and declined her tempting offer for him to stay over. Her house was just a short drive from somewhere he now felt compelled to visit. A bright white moon shone down over the ancient landscape of Cornwall, its light turning the distant sea to glittering black glass. He took the route to a beach he had never visited before, despite its proximity to his childhood home. Parking his car by the top of the cliff, he leaned on the bonnet and breathed in the fresh, salty air. Down below him lay the small beach of pale sand that had been the site of a what he'd always believed was a myth, but which he now knew was the venue of a real event. What good it would do coming here he didn't know, but he needed to see the place with his own eyes, to get as close as he could to the place his father had disappeared from, as if the sand still held some clue he might find.

He picked his way along a narrow path winding down into the cove, the moonlight bright enough for him to see safely. The tide was midway between out and in, and he walked over the soft sand to where the water lapped against the land. Some low rocks were becoming exposed a few metres from the shoreline, disrupting the waves as they broke around them.

It's not suitable for surfing here. The scene was tranquil and quite ordinary, and Toby had no warning when the sea erupted right next to him.

From the water to his left sprang a mermaid, her hands grasping his arm so hard he thought the bone would break. Then to his right another rose up, grabbing his other arm just as forcefully. He cried out and tried to break free but he might as well have tried to escape iron manacles. In the moonlight, he could see his two attackers, who were beautiful and terrifying in equal measure—and almost completely identical. They had long, copper coloured hair that was braided and woven with shells and coral, and though it was hard to tell, they seemed a little older than the maid he had captured. The only difference between the twins was that one bore spiralling green lines across her body and arms, while the other did not. Their perfect faces were grim. Slimy kelp-stem ropes were wound around his neck and wrists, pulled tight to the point where he thought he would choke.

"Let me go!" yelled Toby, still trying to pull away. The maids said nothing but began to drag him forward into the sea, unstoppable and unspeaking, yanking on his bindings. Toby screamed, thrashing his legs as the water rose higher up his body. They were dragging him towards the rocks, their powerful tails churning the black water. Toby was now neck deep and trying to ready himself for what would surely come, when his captors stopped and held him in place. He coughed as a wave broke against his face, inhaling a mouthful of brine. The mermaids were no longer looking at him. Instead, they turned towards the nearest of the rocks, right in front of them.

Upon this stone now sat yet another mermaid. She looked down with a pitiless gaze at the young man shivering in the water—her face as flawless as those of the others. This maid's hair was dark and she wore a necklace of twisted seaweed. And if the two holding him looked angry, this one clearly bore a wrath that could bring down a ship.

"We should drown you, Toby Moore." Her voice was sharp as a blade of ice.

"I'm sorry! I never meant to hurt her," Toby pleaded, his whole body shaking.

"We should drown you," repeated the maid, "but we will not. You and I need to talk. And this time, you will listen."

CHAPTER FOUR

Toby scrambled up the cliff path towards his car, his clothes wringing wet and freezing cold. He slipped and almost fell, but hardly noticed. He had to get back to the warehouse. He had to get back to his mermaid right now. There could be no delay.

He trembled, as much from the shock of what the dark-haired maid had told him as from his rough treatment in the shallows. His bruised arms burned where the twins had gripped him and his throat was sore from the coil they had placed around his neck, but he paid no attention to his discomfort. His perspective on the world had been forcibly shifted—a new truth brought to light—and though his mind kicked and screamed against accepting it, he had no choice.

Dripping over the interior of his car, he started the engine and roared away beyond safe speed along the winding lane leading back to the main road. When he reached it, he accelerated faster still, hoping no police cars were in the area. Fortunately no patrols passed him.

It was half an hour before he reached the MMS warehouse where his prisoner was held. He fumbled to unlock the door with his key, but then realised it was already unlocked. Fritz must be inside. He needed to hear what had happened too. But beyond the door, the room stood in darkness.

He lurched in and switched on the light. The fluorescent tubes flickered for a second then came on steadily. Toby ran to the tank, his heart beating hard and fast.

The tank stood empty. The mermaid was gone.

Toby kept staring, blinking, as if it would somehow make her reappear. He walked right round the tank, like a magician might do to prove the disappearance of a tiger from a cage. But there was no trick here, just an empty cube of salt water. The room was silent, the water filtration system now switched off.

"Fritz. You bastard," he muttered. It had to be Fritz's doing. For a start, he was the only other person with a key to the warehouse. But what had he done with her? Toby's first thought was that the student had released her back into the sea, but then another possibility emerged.

"Yes, I know what you did," he said to the empty room. "You took her to Professor Lindridge, didn't you?" He paced up and down, trying to work out what to do. He pulled out his phone to call Fritz, but it was dead, ruined by its unexpected plunge into the sea. Swearing, he tossed the useless device across the room. He dropped down on the chair by the desk and held his head in his hands, frowning as ideas came to him. Fritz couldn't keep the mermaid in his flat; there wasn't even a bathtub to put her in. He must have taken her to the marine biology department at the university—even at this late hour. He got up and ran back to his car, ready for another drive.

* * * *

Darkness cloaked the university buildings, save for a few security lights, and the muffled thump of dance music issued from the student union building across the road. He parked near the goods entrance for the block housing the biology faculty labs and making sure nobody could see him, he tried the door.

It was locked tight. He'd have to go round the front and try to bluff his way in past whoever was on security tonight. He walked round the perimeter of the building and peeped through the glass doors at the front to see the security desk. He was relieved to see that tonight's guard was Tom, a genial fellow whom Toby had got on very well with during his time as a student. He tapped on the door and Tom looked up, then walked to the door, surprised.

"Toby? Is that you?" he said.

"Uh, yes. Hello there, Tom." The guard immediately unlocked the door and swung it open.

"Good to see you lad. How's life? It must be... what? Two years since you graduated?" He ushered Toby into the building.

"Yes, two years. How are you and Melissa?" He hadn't expected to get in so easily, but he would still have to deal with the matter of gaining access to Abbie Lindridge's lab itself.

"Great, thanks. She's the same as ever, still working the graveyard shifts over at the hospital. It's grand to see you—it's quite the night for unexpected visitors!"

"Oh? How so?"

"Well, a couple of hours ago a student turned up, banging on the door. I was going to tell him to piss off, you know. He looked to me like he'd had a few drinks. He insisted he needed to get in to Professor Lindridge's lab. I told him no way was I going to let a student in there in the middle of the night. He got a bit shirty then he prowled about outside talking to someone on the phone."

"Did he have brown curly hair and a little goatee beard?" asked Toby.

Tom nodded. "That's the fellow. You know him?"

"Yeah. He's Fritz Chadwick. He's one of Abbie's students."

"Ah, right. Anyway, about half an hour later he came back, and the professor was with him. She said it was okay to let him in, and since she was with him, I didn't see why not. It's her lab after all, even if this is an odd time for her to visit. They went in then went back out and brought something in wrapped up in black plastic."

Toby's heart leaped. Tom continued.

"The student fellow left about twenty minutes ago, but the professor's still up there. I'm guessing you're here to help with whatever it is they're up to?"

Toby smiled, hoping his nerves didn't show. Here was his opportunity.

"That's right. Science calls!"

"Well, you go right on up then, lad. I'm fine here with my crosswords to pass the time. It's good to see you. We should go for a drink some time, eh?"

"Yes, that would be nice. See you later, Tom." He offered a silent prayer of thanks that Tom hadn't noticed how wet his clothes still were.

Toby took the lift up to the third floor, where the research labs were located. He reasoned that would be the most likely place to keep the mermaid. He was in luck when he reached the main door to the lab complex, for it needed a key to open, and Lindridge had done it for him. A code lock secured the doors to the individual labs, but Toby remembered the sequence from his student days. It hadn't changed for years. As stealthily as possible, he sneaked in.

He was immediately certain he was in the right place. Lights were on and a computer screen glowed in the corner. He couldn't see anyone about, but he still crept across the room like a cat. As he rounded a tall cabinet he saw her—lying stretched out supine on a table, pale as the moon itself, save for her grey tail and the ugly blotches on her flank.

And this time Toby saw her not with revulsion, not with hatred or thoughts of revenge, but with an emotion he could not describe, for he had never had cause to feel it until now.

* * * *

"You must listen to me, Toby," the dark-haired mermaid had said. "You must listen to what she wanted to say to you, the words you didn't give yourself a chance to hear. And I must tell you how to help her, for you have put her life in grave danger."

"What was she trying to tell me?" he had cried, as the waves splashed against him.

"Your father came to live with me. I was his wife. I loved him with all my soul, and it is only for that reason my sisters and I do not tear you apart this very moment, for I see him in you." Her eyes had sparkled in the dim blue light as she remembered. "The maid you caught… her name is Athina."

"I'm so sorry! I didn't mean to hurt her; it's just that I…"

"You don't know who she is, do you?" The maid had slid off the rock and into the water, her face just inches from Toby's. He could not be sure, but he thought there were tears on her cheek.

"Jonathan and I had a child. She is our daughter."

Toby gulped for breath as the mermaid spoke.

"She is your sister."

* * * *

Toby looked down at her laid out on the table, just as she had been in the warehouse when he and Fritz had measured her, catalogued her, reduced her to facts and figures. He took her hand in his, feeling the coolness of her soft skin.

"Athina," he said, "Can you hear me? It's Toby."

She did not stir. Was she even still alive? He looked

about for something shiny and found a glass beaker, which he held near her mouth. Very faintly, he could see a little condensation forming as she breathed. He watched her face and now became aware of the similarity to his own, revealing the shadow of another face he remembered only from photographs his mother had kept.

He turned suddenly, startled by a noise. Was Professor Lindridge coming back from wherever she had gone? But the sound came from the air conditioning switching on under thermostat control. Still, he had little time to get Athina out of the lab before the professor did show up again.

Toby's attention was attracted by the computer screen, on which was a half-written e-mail. Lindridge was about to share her find with others.

Dear Maurice,
You won't believe what one of the students has just brought me. He rang me at about midnight tonight claiming he had found a new species and demanding I come down to the lab to let him in so he could show me. I thought he was mad or playing a prank or something but he was so insistent I got up and went over there. I was completely blown away. He has captured what appears to be—and I still can't believe I'm really writing this—a mermaid. She's right here in my lab. I'm attaching some photographs. I assure you this is NOT a hoax. This is a real creature and she's still alive, though only just. I'm sorry to say I don't think she will last the night. She's got some abdominal injury and is unconscious. I can't take her to hospital. God knows what would happen. I'm going to try to get some more equipment to see if I can sustain her a little longer.

The message stopped there. That explained where the professor had gone, but her return must undoubtedly be imminent. Toby had to act fast.

Casting around the lab, he found the plastic sheeting Athina had been parcelled in for her journey. With some difficulty, he managed to slide it under her and began to wrap her with great care, leaving it loose around her head so she would not suffocate.

He was about to begin moving her when he remembered something else he couldn't leave behind. He darted back to the computer and checked the e-mail carefully. There were seven photo files attached to the message and he deleted them all, making sure they were completely wiped off the hard drive. The camera lay beside the computer, and he snatched it up and popped out the memory card. There was no telling if she'd copied the images to anywhere else yet, but it was all he could do for now to destroy the evidence of his sister's existence.

Hoisting her in his arms, he struggled out of the door, praying he wouldn't find anyone coming up the corridor. He could hear footsteps far off round a corner, coming closer. It had to be the professor, and he would have a hard time explaining himself if she saw him. He hit the lift call button as fast as he could. The metallic doors opened right away and he dived inside, out of view. A second or two later and he would have been seen. He let out a large sigh as the lift doors closed to conceal him. He hadn't realised he'd been holding his breath.

He exited into the lobby of the building, manoeuvring out of the lift sideways so he didn't catch Athina's head or tail on the doors. Now he must hope Tom wasn't too curious.

The guard looked up from his puzzle.

"That was a quick visit. Is that what I saw them bringing in earlier—a dolphin, is it?" With horror, Toby realised the plastic around Athina's tail had slipped off and her glistening grey fins were hanging out for all to see.

"Uh, yes it's a… dead dolphin calf. We thought it would be useful to study, but… but it's been, er, contaminated. So we need to dispose of it, I'm afraid."

"Eww." Tom pulled a disgusted face as he unlocked the door. "You'd better get it out of here, I suppose. Ought you to be wearing gloves or something?"

"I'll wash my hands really well straight away. G'night Tom!"

Toby's car sped through the night, which soon began to lighten as summer dawn approached. Athina lay limp on the back seat.

"Please don't die. Please don't die," he repeated over and over. His own house was too far to take her and so was the warehouse, but he knew a closer safe haven. It was not long before he pulled in to Priya's driveway. He jabbed the doorbell several times and after a moment, an upstairs light came on. A window opened and a sleepy Priya peeped out.

"You changed your mind then?" she said, yawning.

"Priya, you have to help me. Can you let me in, please?"

"Of course, sweetie. Just a moment. I'll be right down." She soon opened the front door, clutching her dressing gown around her. Toby beckoned her to the car and opened the back door.

"Look," he said.

Priya shrieked and jumped back. For a moment Toby thought she was frightened but then he saw the expression of joy on her face.

"Oh Toby! You were telling the truth. This is amazing. She is *real!*" She hopped up and down excitedly and clapped.

"Yes, she's real, but she's also very sick. We need to get her into your bath. Can you start running one and dump a whole load of salt in, please? Cold, but not too cold."

"Of course, right away." Priya dashed back into the house and up the stairs. Toby lifted his newfound sister from the car and followed, trying not to trip over the cat, which rubbed around his legs. Since he'd found her at the lab, she had not opened her eyes or made any sound, and her breathing was still barely detectable. He kept feeling her neck to check she still had a pulse, which was slow and weak. But then he wasn't sure what qualified as normal for mermaids. She weighed little and he took her up to the bathroom easily, now she was free of plastic wrapping. Priya was still filling the tub with water and had tipped in a whole packet of salt from the kitchen. When the bath was full, he gently laid Athina in it. Once the water supported her body again, she looked a little less pathetic, the sheen returning to the skin of her tail.

"I still can't quite believe this," murmured Priya. "This must be a dream. I'm dreaming it because we talked about mermaids last night. I'm waiting for the Welsh penguins to appear next."

"I assure you it's not a dream, unless I'm sharing it," said Toby, putting his arm around her. "And she's not just any mermaid, either. Did you notice how wet my car seat was?"

"No... hmm, I see your trousers are a bit damp... Oh, you didn't! You could have stopped and found a bush or—"

"Nothing like that!" Toby laughed. "It's sea water. I went to Trelanton Cove earlier tonight... let me tell you the whole story."

They sat on the bathroom floor and Toby began his tale. He explained the letter left by his father, his encounter with Athina aboard the boat, her capture, and his recent meeting with her mother. Priya listened, utterly fascinated.

"I've been such a fool," he said. "I didn't stop to think there would be other mermaids, even when Fritz suggested it. I just assumed this was the one, since she knew who I was. I still don't understand how. And to think her mother took my dad out of love, rather than as a victim..."

"You couldn't have known," said Priya, consoling him. Toby let out a heavy sigh.

"I suppose not. Maybe if I'd believed Dad's note then I might have realised. I still feel stupid. And I'm ashamed of the way I treated her. If she dies, I'll have it on my conscience for the rest of my life. There's something else I need to do as well."

"What's that?"

"Her mother asked how she had been hurt, and I described her injuries. She told me I needed to make medicine for her."

"How do you do that, then? Can she use human drugs?"

"I've no idea, but she told me how to make a natural remedy. She said I need to get something she called cailplena. I didn't know what it was, so she tried to describe it. She said it was a plant that looked like a brown bag. I guess she means sea potato weed. If it's not that, then I'm at a loss to know."

"No time to waste!" Priya jumped up. "It's light enough now. Let me get some proper clothes on and we'll go find some of this stuff. Do you know where it grows?"

"All over the place… you find it sticking to rocks and shells and other seaweed sometimes. Is it safe to leave Athina here?"

"She's not going to get sucked down the plughole, is she?"

* * * *

They took Priya's car to the nearest rocky beach and began combing for the sea potato weed. At first they found none, but as the tide withdrew and exposed more rocks, so they began to find small patches of the odd leathery weed, like little withered balloons. They collected as much as Toby thought they would need and made haste back to the house. Athina lay exactly as she had been when they had left her.

"What are we supposed to do with it now?" Priya asked.

Toby stroked his chin as he recalled the maid's instructions. "I think we grind it into a paste, and smear it on her bruised areas."

"Right. I've got a mortar and pestle in the kitchen. We can use that."

The brown weed disintegrated easily as they ground it up, turning into a revolting tan coloured slime. They looked apprehensively at the foul pulp and shooed away the cat for trying to eat it.

That animal really has no taste.

"Is this really going to work if we just rub it on her tummy?" Priya was sceptical.

"What else can we do? It's this or nothing. Her mother said simply to apply it like ointment and it would heal her."

They let a little water out of the bath so the paste would not be washed off and daubed it over the dark blotches on Athina's body. It stuck easily to her skin. She did not move as they rubbed it in.

"And now we wait," said Toby, "and if it's all right with you, I'd like to have a bit of sleep."

CHAPTER FIVE

Priya awakened Toby, softly saying his name as she peeped in through her bedroom door. He rubbed his bleary eyes and propped himself up on his elbows.

"What time is it?"

"Just after two in the afternoon," she said. "And guess what? Your sister is awake!"

Toby jumped up, almost losing his balance, and stumbled across the landing to the bathroom. Athina opened her eyes as he came in and smiled weakly. The bruises had already begun to fade as the seaweed remedy took effect, although it was obvious she remained fragile.

"Hello, brother. I hope I should be pleased to see you again." Her voice was still hoarse and thin.

"I... I'm so sorry. Forgive me, I..." Toby trailed off, looking down at the floor.

"I have been talking to Priya. She told me what has been happening." Athina winced a little as she shifted position in the bathtub. "I was frightened when I awoke here. The last thing I can remember is you feeding me—then nothing. There are things we must speak of, but now... I need to rest a while longer." She closed her eyes again and settled back in the water. Toby slipped out onto the landing and closed the bathroom door.

Downstairs in the kitchen, Priya had made coffee. The bright sun made the day seem cheerful outside the window as they sat and sipped.

"I did offer her some clothes, by the way. She said she didn't need them," said Priya, almost apologetically. "It must be weird to have your sister going around like that."

"Oh, like it's not weird she has a tail and lives under the sea?" Toby grinned and stretched his arms behind his head, gazing out at the peaceful countryside beyond the window.

"I wonder what's happened to Fritz?"

"Oh, he's probably going bananas right now. And Abbie Lindridge too. I suspect the only reason we haven't heard from him is that my phone's busted, and he doesn't know where I am. And I hope poor Abbie never got as far as telling anyone what she had. She'd be a laughing stock, and I wouldn't wish that on her."

"Will you tell your mum about this?"

"It's better not to. I don't think she could cope with the truth. She made the choice not to believe it years ago and it's kinder to let her go on with that. Besides, confirming your husband wasn't insane but did actually fall in love with someone else is never going to go down well."

"The other mermaids you saw… and her mother… were they as pretty as she is?" Priya's voice betrayed her envy.

"Yes. They looked older than Athina, of course, but younger than they probably are. I don't know how long they live for, but Athina can't be more than twenty-two at the oldest. Assuming she was conceived after Dad left, that is."

"She's the most beautiful woman I've ever seen. I feel like a dumpling next to her."

Toby leaned over and hugged her tightly. "I think you are way better looking. For a start, you've got nicer legs."

DEEP SECRETS

* * * *

At about ten o'clock at night, sounds of movement from the bathroom alerted them that their patient was awake again. They knocked on the bathroom door and peered in. They had left a dish of sardines by the side of the tub in case the mermaid wanted to eat, and Athina was now helping herself to them. Her face brightened with a smile as the two land-folk entered.

"Are those okay? I wasn't sure what you liked," said Priya. Athina nodded.

"These are delicious! My favourite fish," she replied. Her voice had strengthened, regaining some of the pure clarity Toby had heard her speak with at their first meeting. She licked her lips and turned to face Toby.

"If you had let me speak to you as I wanted to, things would have been better," she said, her tone laced with disapproval. She swallowed another piece of sardine and continued. "I came to you as a friend and a sister. Mother had told me about you, and one day she happened to see you on your boat, though you did not see her. She knew straight away you were Jonathan's son. She said you look very much like him. And I wanted to meet you... no other maids of my clan have brothers that they know of. Finding you was a most exciting event!"

Toby, feeling chastened, looked down at the floor. Athina finished off the last sardine and rolled over in the tub, flexing her tail fin like a fan.

"Mother warned me land-men could be dangerous, but she also knew that our father left a message for you. It had to be passed on, and I was eager to do it. That is why I came to you, in peace."

"I have to ask," he replied, "although I think I know the answer from the way you and your mother talk about him. Is my father... our father... is he dead?"

Athina nodded, her expression wistful.

"Yes. He left this world some seventeen years ago. My

memory of him is vague, sadly, but such is the way with my kind. I remember he loved me—and Mother. She has taken no other husband since."

"I have no memory of him at all." Loneliness washed over Toby, despite the presence of his sister and girlfriend. There was no love left for him from his father. It had gone to these strange, underwater people—and he had been rejected.

"What was the message?" asked Priya, unable to restrain her curiosity. Athina shrugged, a strangely human gesture that looked odd on a mermaid.

"We do not know. He wrote it in your language, and while we speak it well enough, we cannot read or write it."

"I see." Toby frowned as he thought. "So it must be physically located somewhere. Can we see it?"

"Yes… and no," said the mermaid. "It is in a place impossible for land-folk to reach without the aid of one of my kind. I had always intended to take you there, but I am still too weak."

The bruising had continued to fade but remained quite visible. It was clear Athina's condition made her too vulnerable to return to the sea just yet, but it was impractical keeping her in the bath with no room to move—and besides, Priya would need to wash eventually. The three of them discussed various options and decided the most sensible course was to return her to the big tank in the MMS warehouse. At first, Athina was nervous, for the tank held unpleasant memories as much as water, but when they assured her there would be no tying up involved and that Priya would also come with them when they brought her there, she was a little happier with the idea.

They carried her downstairs and out to Toby's car then loaded an air mattress and some bedding into the boot. Athina was fearful of being left in the warehouse on her own and Toby also thought it wise to have a round-the-clock watch, in case Fritz attempted any more abductions.

Athina stared out of the car window as they drove, amazed to see the constructions of the land-folk and their many wonders. They had insisted she wear a t-shirt for the journey to preserve herself from the stares of anyone looking into the car from the outside.

"This is incredible. I never realised there were so many strange things on the land!" she said. "We do not build so much in our home as you do."

They found the warehouse much as Toby had left it, though he knew without a doubt that Fritz must have come by at some point to find his missing prize. The tank was still full, and Athina stretched out gracefully, swimming loops and twirling through the water, a lovely contrast to her previous semi-comatose occupancy. She requested they supply a coarse net, with one edge weighted down. Toby managed to rig up the net he had used to capture her to meet the requirements, although its purpose mystified him. He soon found out that with the top edge tied near the rim of the tank, Athina could wind her arms through the holes and was thus held in place to sleep, with her head out of the water.

"At home, we have webbing made from seaweed for this purpose, inside the air caves," she explained. Priya pumped up the airbed and made it as cosy as she could for Toby and herself, and the three of them slept until dawn.

Over the next few days, Athina recovered her former strength. She still slept for long periods but when she was awake, she was lively and chatty, constantly questioning Toby about all aspects of land life. Priya came by often, though she had to fit in her visits around work at the cafe. She and the mermaid had formed a definite bond of friendship. Toby replaced his ruined phone and called the MMS, apologising for missing several shark tag calls and explaining he would be out of work for a while due to family illness. It was technically true, after all.

It wasn't long before Fritz showed up. Toby was

talking to Athina, sitting on the stepladder by the tank, when the door opened a crack and Fritz's furtive face poked through. On seeing Toby there, he froze for a moment then swaggered in, trying to look nonchalant. Toby got off the ladder to meet him.

"Hello, Toby. I see you have our mermaid back in the tank." Toby glanced up at Athina, who had closed her eyes and lay as still as she had been when injured.

"Yes, there she is. No thanks to you."

"I don't know what you're talking about. I just came here to find her gone the other day," Fritz lied. "I tried calling you but you didn't answer."

"My phone was broken. And I know perfectly well what you got up to. Tom, on security, told me."

Fritz's face reddened at being found out, and his tone became surly.

"I suppose you aren't going to admit stealing her out of the lab? Abbie blamed me for that, you know," he said.

Toby raised an eyebrow. "I didn't steal her any more than you did."

"Ah, no—not true," said Fritz, wagging a finger. "She was partly my property. So I can do what I like with her."

"She's nobody's property!" snorted Toby. "And if I hadn't taken her out of the lab, she'd be dead by now, and in all probability dissected or preserved in formaldehyde by Professor Lindridge."

"You've changed your tune a bit. I thought you were on a revenge trip against her? Didn't she kill your father, you said?"

"I was… mistaken. Things aren't what I assumed them to be." Toby didn't want to explain the whole story to Fritz. He still felt guilty over the way he'd treated his sister and had apologised to her endlessly. For her part, Athina was very forgiving and didn't appear to harbour a grudge against him.

"After all," she had said, "if you have a primitive understanding of the world, you're going to have a primitive reaction to it, aren't you? And you didn't even know maids like me existed. A primitive understanding indeed!"

Fritz had begun to ascend the stepladder to get a better view of Athina. She remained motionless as he looked her over.

"I see her bruising has cleared up," he observed. "Did that happen by itself or did you do something to help?"

"Oh... it just faded away." Toby kept expecting Athina to open her eyes and move, or for Fritz to comment on the netting in the tank, but neither happened. Fritz stared at Athina briefly then descended the ladder.

"You know, I still think it would be well worth revealing her to people. And if you don't agree with that, then there's not much you can do about it, right...?" Fritz paused, his implication clear. He didn't want to be denied his glory, even now.

Toby remained unruffled. He'd expected this, and knew how to handle it.

"Didn't Abbie Lindridge have any evidence to show the world herself, then?" he asked, in as innocent a voice as he could manage.

"You know as well as I do what happened to the photos we took in the lab—completely wiped from the computer. All copies gone." Fritz glowered at Toby.

"Mmm... I'm glad to hear it. And it wasn't a good idea to use your camera to take those pictures anyway."

"What do you mean?"

Toby gave a cynical smile. "I'd assumed it was Abbie's camera I took the memory card from. Then when I looked through the files on it, I realised it was yours. There are some very... I should say, *interesting* photos on there."

Fritz went white. Toby continued.

"It's quite lucky Abbie never saw the photos of herself you left on there—you know, the ones of her sunbathing on the beach? I'd imagine you had to use quite a long lens to get them. Technically accomplished photography, but also rather creepy and stalkerish, don't you think? It would be a pity if she somehow came across them."

Fritz hung his head, silent. Toby knew there would be no talk of mermaids from him anymore.

"Well, I guess you have it all under control," Fritz said. "If she wakes up and you need any help…" He trailed off, realising Toby wasn't going to bring him back into the team again. "I'll be seeing you then," he said, turning to walk away. The door closed behind him.

"I think we're better off without him assisting us, don't you?" Toby said. Athina opened her eyes and leaned over the edge of the tank.

"Don't be smug, brother. Fritz wasn't the one who insisted I be tied up—or the one who jabbed me with a dart." She rubbed the spot on her tail where it had pierced her, now fully healed. "He was actually quite kind to me."

"Right up until he took you away to be cut up for research, yes," he reminded her.

"Let's not be drawn into a debate on the moral high tide here. Let's just forgive and forget."

Athina was now confident she was well enough to return to the ocean and to bring Toby to see his father's message.

"Will I need to travel by boat?" he asked, curious to know where they would be going.

"No. A boat cannot go there. We could get near, but not all the way. We must swim from the nearest beach."

"Okay. And which beach is that?"

"Oh!" Athina stopped to think. "I don't know what you call it or how to find it from land—only what it looks like from the sea. It's on the north coast, but… that is many miles long. Perhaps you have seen the place we are going to—two rocks rising from the water, one to a very great height? We call them the Sacred Rocks, but I don't know the land-folk's name for them."

Toby thought of every north coast beach he'd been

on, everywhere he'd surfed, anything that could be what she described. Abruptly it came to him.

"Bawden Rocks! It has to be."

CHAPTER SIX

At dawn's first light, Toby carried Athina across the sand of the beach directly opposite Bawden Rocks. They stood two miles out to sea, farther than Toby could swim and even if he could, lethal currents might sweep him far out into the ocean. He was dressed in his surfing wetsuit, for so early on a summer morning, the air held the night's chill. Not another soul was around at this time.

Toby placed Athina down at the water's edge, and she wriggled into it, visibly pleased at returning to her natural environment.

"Are you ready, brother?" She looked up at him, and he took a step into the surf towards her.

"I am. Let's go." He waded a little deeper then placed his hands on her shoulders and his legs astride her tail.

"Very well. Hang on tight!" With a swish of her tail, Athina launched them out into the water. Toby was astonished by her speed and received a non-stop spray of seawater in his face as they raced along, for he was just above the surface. Athina herself swam just beneath it, occasionally bobbing her head up and taking a noisy breath. After a while, Toby's face began to sting from its battering and he tapped Athina's shoulder to get her to stop.

"Are you all right?" Athina was a little amused at his discomfort, though not unkindly.

"Yeah, I'm fine. My face just needs a break. I feel like I'm being towed by a jet ski!"

"Try lying a little flatter, and place your hands farther down—about here." Athina indicated an area on her torso, just above her waist.

"Oh, right—on the lines?" he asked

"Yes. That's a good way to keep them in the right place."

Toby suddenly remembered a difference he'd seen between Athina and her mother—and in one of the other mermaids.

"These lines on your body... why do some mermaids have them and not others? What are they, some sort of camouflage?"

A full minute passed before Athina stopped laughing enough to be able to answer the question, while Toby bobbed in the water, looking confused.

"They're tattoos, silly! Did you think we had these patterns naturally? Oh, that's so funny!"

"Well, I wasn't to know, was I?" he replied.

"No, I suppose not. Mother doesn't like them and scolded me dreadfully when I got them done, but I'm nineteen now so I can do what I like!" She flashed a rebellious smile.

Maybe mermaids and humans are more alike than different. Toby considered the thought. It came to him as quite a surprise.

They continued on their journey for another mile before they came to the foot of the towering rocks. The largest rose to over eighty feet above them, its summit occupied by razorbills and gulls. Local legend said this hill in the sea had been thrown there by a giant.

"This is it? Do we have to climb up there?" Toby didn't like the idea of scaling the vertical island.

"No. We go down."

"Down?" Now he was even more worried.

"Hold on to me tightly," Athina said, "and whatever you do, don't let go. And make sure you get a good breath of air before we dive. You might find this a little hard on you."

Down they went, Toby clinging on as best he could around his sister's slim waist. He opened his eyes but could see little of their dim surroundings as they plunged ever deeper. The pressure hurt his ears then his lungs began to protest, demanding fresh air. He held on, using all his strength and concentration to resist the urge to let go and fight upwards. The seconds passed slowly as the need for air became unbearable, though they were no longer moving down. Toby couldn't take any more—he had to let go.

As he did, his head broke the surface.

They were in a cave of overwhelming size inside the rock. A beam from a hole high above lit the patches of moss and lichen decorating the walls of this natural cathedral. Copper deposits within the grey stone marked it with vivid streaks of peacock blue.

"This is amazing. I never knew this rock was hollow." Toby panted and gasped as he took in the scene.

"Most land-men don't. Some divers visit the outside, but the passage in here is hidden. You did well to hold your breath." Athina guided him to a broad ledge where he could climb out of the water, and she clambered up to join him. They sat in peaceful silence for a few minutes while Toby recovered then Athina reached up to a crack in the wall.

From the crack, she withdrew a large piece of slate, holding it reverently.

"Father came here sometime in the first few days he was with us and wrote this. He told Mother that if she ever found you, she should pass it on." She handed the slate to Toby.

Etched upon its surface were words, grown faint in the

twenty-three years since they had been inscribed, but still legible. Toby held the slate up to catch the dim sunlight and read the message.

My dear Toby,

I don't know when—or if—you will see this. My life has changed so much, yet as I write this, yours has just begun. You must understand that what I did, choosing to follow my maidwife as one of the merfolk, was not an easy decision for me, even though she has given me more love than anyone in my life ever has. The one thing I regret leaving behind is you. I will never see you take your first steps or hear you say your first word. I will never see you off for your first day at school—or your last.

I could not bear for you to think I didn't care about you. I wanted to be a better father, but it was so difficult for me. There was a wall between your mother and I that I could never find a way to cross, and she kept you just beyond my reach. But I never stopped reaching, never stopped trying to be the best I could, and whatever happens to me, there will be a part of my heart I know will love you until its last beat.

It may be hard for you to understand my reasons. Perhaps you never will, but I can only ask you to forgive my failings. You will always be my son, and nothing can compare to you.

Love always,
Daddy

Athina put a hand on Toby's shoulder as a tear trickled down his face. He leaned back against the stone of the cave and closed his eyes.

"Is it bad news?" his sister asked. Toby shook his head.

"No. Good news. News that helps." He put his arms around her and gave her a hug.

"Thank you," he whispered.

Brother and sister left the cave a while later, emerging to bright morning sunshine. They travelled back to the beach and sat together on the sand.

"Are you still going to write about me in your papers,

as you had planned to?" Athina asked. Toby shook his head.

"Of course not. I wanted to claim the glory of revealing the merfolk to the world, but all it would do is endanger you. When I didn't care, it didn't matter, but now I'd rather not let everyone know."

"The land world has always known of my kind." The young mermaid smiled as she gazed out to sea. "They just don't want to let themselves believe it. One day there will come a time. But not yet." She looked about, anxious. "I shouldn't stay long. Other people might come here."

"I guess so." Sadness touched him when he thought of her leaving, but he knew she was taking a little bit of the land back with her, just as he would now always be joined to the sea. Athina slid down into the foam that washed the beach.

"I'll keep in touch!" she called, waving her tail fin to Toby, and with a flick, she submerged.

Just for a moment as the shadow of a cloud dimmed the sun's glare from the water, he was sure he saw other maids there, swirling and spiralling up from the depths, joining his sister and welcoming her as she made her way home.

SEAGULL'S EXILE

CHAPTER ONE
Birth and Death

In the cave beneath the water, the only light came from the pinpoint blue stars of the immobile creatures lining the walls. Dim, but easily enough for the sensitive eyes of the two mermaids to see their surroundings.

Morveren clutched her belly as the muscles tightened again.

"She is coming soon. It feels the same as last time."

Her sister, Delen, stroked Morveren's creased brow, soothing her. She relaxed and floated upwards to the roof of the cave to take a fresh breath of air. Delen swam with her and they rested with their heads above the surface. Morveren already had three pretty daughters and soon the family would grow by one more.

Morveren's emotions were an equal mix of joy at the forthcoming arrival and grief at the loss of another whom she loved. The waiting agonised her. With each passing hour, the chance of hearing news of her husband's return diminished. She had to accept that. No man could last forever here, but reminding herself of this fact did nothing to dull the pain of parting.

Delen could tell where her sister's thoughts were centred.

"You know they have scouts looking out for Pierre right now. There is still hope he may come back."

"There is little hope, and it decreases still. He is gone."

"All men must pass on to the next world. But Pierre has left you with four beautiful daughters. Well, nearly four."

Morveren thought of her children—identical twins Kensa and Tamon, five years old, who shared their father's soulful brown eyes. Then Kerra, only three, with her bright smile so like his. And as if to remind her, Morveren felt another squeeze inside and a responding push back from the as yet unnamed maid within. Would she resemble her father as well?

The hour grew late, and still attended by Delen, Morveren slipped into sleep. But not for long, as the contractions continued to strengthen, making further rest impossible. She circled the cave, frequently rising to the air pocket in the roof to take deep breaths.

"How are you feeling? Should I get Senara, just in case?" asked Delen, concerned. But Morveren shook her head. She didn't need the attention of the clan's wise one for this birth, instinctively sure there would be no major problems.

"No. I'll be fine. Just stay with me."

"Of course." Delen held her hand, ready to provide what comfort she could.

The waves of pain increased, and the passage of time was difficult for Morveren to gauge.

"She's coming!" she heard Delen say, "I can see the top of her head!"

More contractions, ever stronger, then a hard push and suddenly everything eased as the baby's shoulders were out and the rest of her tiny streamlined body floated free. Morveren leaned back, gasping as Delen scooped up the baby, who wriggled in her newfound freedom of open water.

"Your daughter… and my new niece!" said Delen,

smiling broadly. Morveren held the infant close, keeping her head above the water so she could take her first breath. The baby swivelled her eyes about, not yet able to see anything clearly, and sucked in a big lungful of air. Then she blew it back out again strongly, her diminutive ribcage almost flattening. She repeated this process two or three more times, and Morveren knew the little one would be able to hold her breath well enough to swim. The baby had no hair yet, and her eye colour was hard to determine in the cave's faint light. She flapped her tiny light-grey tail against her mother's arm and gave a small cry. She was hungry.

Morveren fed her while Delen left the cave to break the news to the rest of the clan. A few minutes later she returned—with company.

"Mother! Are you all right? Can we see her, please?" Kensa rushed up to her mother, eager to greet the latest family member, swiftly followed by Tamon and Kerra, who crowded round the startled infant.

"Now girls, don't frighten her. She can't see well and things are strange to her."

"What's her name?" asked Kerra.

"She doesn't have a name yet. She won't have one until she is a year old, when we know what name would suit her best."

"Can we call her Starfish?" suggested Kerra.

Tamon tutted at her younger sibling. "You want to call everything Starfish. That's what you called all your dolls."

Morveren laughed. "No, she won't be called that. Just wait and see. Be patient. Now, let's take her out so everyone else can meet her, shall we?"

The maids swam down the short entrance tunnel of the cave, emerging to the broad, sandy area outside. Above, the full moon cast its light into the shallow water. Several other maids and men waited there, all delighted to see Morveren and her baby emerge safely. After the inevitable cooing over the newborn, they escorted her back to the village a short distance away. Only now did Morveren realise how exhausted she was. She would sleep soundly and her children should also be resting. It was very late for them.

They approached the entrance to the air caves in which they made their homes. Stretching down deep into the sea from the face of a sheer cliff above, the stone wall contained openings to natural passageways within the rock, allowing fresh air to circulate from above. Within, there was enough space for the whole clan to sleep in several chambers. Areas not directly linked to the air passages were supplied with bubbles brought down in sheets of shark hide, until they too had a breathing space within them. As with the small birthing cave, lighting came from phosphorescent sea creatures brought up from the deep water.

As a new mother, Morveren was allocated a cosy family chamber within the caves where she could take care of her baby in private, although she also knew it was to prevent the baby from waking the other residents if she should cry during the night. Entering, she felt the emotional stab of how it was different to the last time she gave birth, three years ago. On that occasion, her husband had been with her. But this baby would never know her father. Morveren clung to her last link to him, a fragile life, so tiny but with so much potential in her future.

Pierre had become difficult over the last few weeks. He could not remember things clearly, and it had made him frustrated, which then turned to anger. He never directed it at others, but would go off on his own for hours, not speaking. He had begun to have trouble remembering his daughter's names then got lost trying to find his way out of the caves and nearly drowned. The rapid decline had shocked his wife. The smiling, intelligent land-man she had taken to join her world had gone, replaced by a dark, moody stranger. But he had been lucky to survive as a merman for six years; Delen's husband had lasted only two before he had succumbed to the confusion of the Dark Change and swam down to the depths. The price the landmen paid for joining the merfolk was the loss of their minds and then their lives. And the price paid by the maidwives was to always lose those they loved.

"Mother, we can stay up and look after her for you," said Kensa hopefully.

Morveren laughed and kissed her daughter's copper-haired head. "No, you can't. You should have been asleep hours ago. Now close your eyes, for this one may yet wake you!"

"Hmm, if she's like Kerra was as a baby, she'll scream all the time," said Tamon, pouting.

"Hush now. Kerra did not scream. If anything, you were the noisiest of the lot," chided her mother. She looked over at Kerra, who was already nodding off, her arms entwined through the seaweed ropes that stopped them from drifting away while they slept. "Now follow your sister's example and go to your dreams."

Cradling her newborn in her arms, Morveren began to sing a gentle lullaby, until all her daughters were asleep.

****

In the morning, although there was joy at the baby's arrival, there was also sadness at Pierre's absence. The scouts who had gone to search for him came back and broke the news to Morveren that they had seen him descending towards the deeper waters of the west, beyond where they could follow. That meant he could no longer be alive.

But there was a new life to teach about the world and much yet to be done. Today the baby's blessing ceremony would happen. Leaving the other girls in Delen's care, she took the baby to meet with Senara.

The wise one of the clan was afforded the privilege of her own garden area, where she tended weeds and creatures used for medicine and charms. A short swim from the air caves, the well-tended garden was a delightful spot. When Morveren was a girl, Senara had jet black hair, but now age had turned it mostly white, with only an occasional dark streak recalling its former glory.

"Welcome, Morveren!" called Senara as they approached, laying down her basket of seaweed where it would not be taken by a current. "Oh my, she is so beautiful!" she exclaimed on seeing the infant. Morveren carried her carefully, guiding her along facing forwards, as if swimming for real. Although technically able to swim and hold her breath, it would be another couple of weeks before the baby could control her direction of movement and even then, a slight eddy in the water could send her tumbling.

They rose to the surface to talk. The cloudless weather brought a bright day up above, and the baby blinked in the sunshine, surprised. This was the first time she had seen the sky.

"How are you feeling, my dear?" The older maid laid a hand on Morveren's belly, checking that all felt as it should. She was also the clan's midwife and had helped Morveren throughout her pregnancy.

"Fine," she replied. "A trifle sore, but not nearly as bad as after the twins."

Senara chuckled. "Well, you had a rough birth that time, no mistake." She turned her attention to the baby. "Any concerns? Is she feeding well? Holding her breath properly?"

"Oh, yes. She's a hungry little thing. Her breath holding is good, I think. She doesn't cry much, but she does squeak a lot!" As if on cue, the girl let out a high pitched squeal at a seagull floating on the water nearby. The gull gave her a disgusted look and flew off. The other maids laughed. Senara gave the baby a long stare, as if seeing something her mother could not. Then she turned back to Morveren.

"We shall have her blessing this afternoon. I will go and prepare the Circle right away."

****

Morveren had decorated her newest daughter with a fine necklace made of sea grass and slivers of mussel shell. She and Delen, accompanied by the three older children, made their way to Senara's garden. In an area where no plants were cultivated, Senara had prepared a circle of several different objects—a glistening white crystal, a piece of wood from the land, a branch of coral, and other things. The wise one waited inside this circle, smiling as they approached.

"Welcome, daughter of Morveren," said Senara as they arrived, directly addressing the baby. "You are here to receive the blessing of long life and health."

Morveren handed the slightly drowsy baby to Senara, who laid her carefully in the centre of the circle. The infant rested peacefully on the sand, unconcerned. Senara held a crab carapace in her hand, its surface etched with symbols. She leaned close to the baby and touched the shell gently against her forehead.

"May you be granted wisdom to help you in times of trouble," said the wise one. She moved the shell and touched it to the baby's tail fin. "May you be granted swiftness to help you in times of danger." She moved the shell to the baby's chest. "And may you be granted love, that you shall know its joy." She raised the crab shell above the baby and with a swift movement, crushed it between her hands. Fragments rained down in the circle, some landing on the tiny figure lying within it. She, however, had drifted off to sleep.

"Go now, and return in one year to receive your name," said Senara, motioning for Morveren to retrieve her daughter.

"We want to call her Starfish," said Kerra solemnly.

Senara laughed. "You might want to, my dear, but I suspect your mother may have other names in mind!"

****

Ten months passed, and Morveren's baby grew strong and healthy. She swam fast for her age, her hair was growing a rich chestnut brown, and although she could not yet speak, she showed an amazing capability with imitation. She copied noises she heard, especially the cries of gulls and other birds. They fascinated her, and she loved to spend time at the surface, trying to reach for the birds as they swooped above her. Morveren took her ashore frequently with the other children, where she splashed happily in rock pools and played gently with the transparent shrimp as they darted around her. She could not move on land at all yet—that skill was rare before about three years—and Kerra was just beginning to master the coordination required to slither across the sand or shingle easily. Her older sisters used this to their advantage, teasing their younger sibling and then dashing away from her faster than she could manage.

The children accompanied their mother when she went to work at the kelp fields each day. Though they had no official responsibility to assist, most young maids helped their mothers with their work as soon as they were old enough to do so, the exception being those maids who patrolled the dangerous area of the Shelf, guarding against predators such as sharks and hunting larger, stronger fish with their spears. Tamon and Kensa were already quite good at harvesting the smaller varieties of kelp the clan cultured. Kerra was still too young to contribute and spent most of her time minding her younger sister. She splashed about at the surface with the baby, far above her mother and older sisters. Morveren could not count how many times in a day she glanced upwards to check the pair was still there and tended to work as close to the surface as she could, just in case.

On one such day, she received a visit from Delen. Delen was not a farmer, but a weaver. She worked with others to construct the fine nets of sea grass used to catch smaller fish. These nets were not robust, and the work of making new ones and repairing the ones in use never ceased.

Delen looked up at Kerra and the baby splashing merrily at the surface above them.

"Not long now until she must have her name. Have you decided yet?"

Normally maids did not reveal their chosen name for their daughters until a full year had elapsed, but Morveren did not mind confiding in her sister.

"Yes. She's decided it for me, really. Do you hear that?"

Delen cocked her head, listening to the happy shrieks her niece was making. She raised an eyebrow. "She's very good at mimicking those birds, isn't she? And I've heard her do porpoise calls too, I'm sure."

"Oh yes," Morveren nodded, "and many other sounds. But it's the birds she loves. She's fascinated with them. I think she wants to be one! So I decided her name should be Zethar."

Delen nodded in agreement. "Of course... it means seagull. Perfect for her!"

CHAPTER TWO
The Song of the Dolphin

Zethar darted among the rock pillars, swimming as close as she could without grazing herself on their rough edges. She dared not glance behind her, knowing her pursuer would catch her if she slowed even slightly. She spun downwards, making for a concealed channel in the rock, but she was spotted and twisted round to power upwards, making for the top of one of the stony columns. But her shoulder snagged an outcrop, knocking the breath from her and stunning her for a moment. Clutching her injured arm, she attempted to struggle up for air. But her lead was lost and her pursuer had won. A hand swiped against her tail fin.

"Got you!" said the other girl, triumphant. "Your turn to catch me... Oh, are you hurt?"

"I hit my shoulder, Rozen," said Zethar. "I need air." The two girls rose to the surface. A thin trickle of dark blood trailed from Zethar's shoulder where the rock had grazed the skin. Rozen inspected it.

"Zethi, it looks painful. Are you sure you're all right?" Rozen was seven, nearly a year older than Zethar, and if she was concerned, then it worried the younger girl. In truth, the pain was increasing and she tried not to cry.

"Do you think I should go and see Senara?" Zethar's voice trembled.

Rozen nodded. "Yes. She can help you. Come on, let's go right away." Rozen had just begun her training as Senara's acolyte. In time, when Rozen was a grown woman and Senara passed away, she would become the next wise one of the clan.

They dived back down and headed for Senara's garden, which was not too far. The wise one was there, chatting to a couple of other maids, but broke off from them on seeing the youngsters approaching.

"Why, Zethar, whatever is the matter? How did this happen?" Senara rushed to inspect the grazed limb.

"We were playing out by the stone arches and I crashed into one." Zethar looked ashamed.

"Well, accidents happen. Can you turn your arm this way? How about… ah, maybe not." She stopped working the arm as Zethar yelped in pain at one particular movement. She touched the shoulder carefully in a couple of other places then nodded as if confirming her thoughts.

"Right, it's come out of the socket. I will need to put it back in," said Senara. Zethar felt a knot of fear tighten inside her at the thought. Rozen looked terrified. Senara saw her apprehension and spoke comfortingly.

"Don't worry. I shall give you some minnarin extract to reduce the pain and cailplena to stop any bruising inside. You'll be as lithe as an octopus two days from now."

"Can you go and get Mother first, please?" asked Zethar quietly. But Senara shook her head.

"There isn't time to delay. The sooner this is treated, the quicker it will heal. Now Rozen, this is a good chance for you to learn how to do this. Make your friend comfortable on the sand over there. That's good. Do you need to get a breath first?"

"No, I'm fine," replied the injured maid, although she didn't feel fine at all. Senara placed some ground up substance under her tongue.

"Now suck gently on that. The pain will begin to ease," instructed the wise one. Zethar did as she was told and within a minute, she began to feel light-headed. The pain had indeed lessened, and Senara held her arm gently.

"Watch how I do this, Rozen, and hold her other hand." Senara's voice sounded far away as the minnarin continued to increase in effect. Then came a sharp twist and a stab of stronger pain in the shoulder. Zethar cried out, but then the pain diminished as rapidly as it had come.

"There. That should be all right. We'll need to see to the skin though. Rozen, please fetch the cailplena from my store and we'll take her home."

They swam to the air caves, Senara guiding the still intoxicated Zethar. Rozen followed behind. Entering the caves, they swam to the largest central chamber where they could access a space above the water level. The older maid helped the girl up out onto the stone ledge above the water and took a small pouch from Rozen. After instructing her acolyte to go find Morveren and tell her what had happened, Senara removed some thick paste from the pouch and smeared it over Zethar's grazed shoulder. It stung, but soon began to reduce the pain even more.

"Now you stay here, my dear. Your mother should be coming soon."

"Thank you, Senara. I feel... I feel very sleepy."

"Yes, that's the minnarin. A couple of hours will pass before it wears off. Stay here on the ledge. *Don't* go into the water; you may drown."

"I'll stay here. I feel much better already. Senara... one day I'd like to learn to help people, like you do. Can I do that?"

The older maid smiled. "I already have Rozen as my acolyte. She's the one I'm passing my knowledge on to."

"Yes, but Rozen is my friend. We could learn together. Why can't you teach us both?" Zethar's drugged state led her to voice every thought. Senara contemplated the idea.

"Well... traditionally there is only one wise one in the clan. But yes, I don't see why I can't teach you as well. Rozen has only been learning for a few weeks, so you will soon catch up with her. Let me discuss it with your mother though."

Zethar's eyes began to close. She could no longer feel any pain in her shoulder.

"Thank you," she said, and fell asleep.

****

Over the following months, Zethar took her first steps along the path of knowledge. At first the clan was rather surprised when Senara announced she was taking on another acolyte. After all, there had only ever been one trained at a time for as long as anyone knew. There were rumours that other clans in distant waters might have other customs, but in the waters of Kernow it was highly unusual. But Senara's judgement was not questioned, and her suggestion that it may one day be useful to have two wise ones in the clan did bear some merit. It delighted Rozen to have her best friend learning alongside her, and Morveren was quite proud. To have one's daughter chosen as an acolyte was a mark of status. Only Rozen's mother seemed irked at no longer being unique in that regard.

Senara had her own small cave not far from her garden where her lessons took place and where she produced some of her medicines and charms. The work of a wise one was hard and time consuming. A great deal of the day was spent foraging for ingredients, such as particular types of seaweed or a species of animal yielding a necessary product. Zethar and Rozen learned where to look for these things, how to utilise them in various compounds, and what those compounds were used for. In addition, Senara taught them the rituals of the merfolk. The ceremonies of birth blessing, death, marriage, and others had to be conducted with precision if they were to fulfil their function and bring luck or safe passage to the next world.

When Zethar had just turned ten years old, she was out with Rozen in an area far to the east of the area where the clan resided. They were collecting a type of clam found there, which Senara used to make a medicine for easing sickness.

"Look there, Zethi," said Rozen. "Do you see those caves?"

Zethar peered through the dark blue water in the direction her friend pointed.

"Yes," she said. "What's in there?"

"They used to be the air caves our clan lived in, years ago. Senara told me so."

"Really? Why did they move from here?"

Rozen swam closer, beckoning for her friend to follow. She continued the story while they swam.

"Senara said the passages became unsafe. Rocks fell inside and killed a maid and a man. They worried it would happen again, so these caves were abandoned."

Zethar surveyed the black opening uncertainly. The dark rock of the cliff gave the cave a foreboding, unwelcoming look. Weeds swayed in front of the entrance. Rozen continued to drift closer, her blonde hair bright against the sinister hole, but Zethar hung back.

"Don't go in there, Roz! I don't like it."

Rozen turned and laughed.

"Scared?" she asked. "There's nothing to be frightened of. Unless you think there are ghosts in there..."

The thought chilled Zethar. "There might be ghosts. You said people died."

"I'm not afraid of ghosts. They can't touch us. I think I might go in, you know." Rozen boldly flipped her fin, propelling herself to within a metre of the gap. Zethar didn't move.

"Ha ha, you *are* afraid!" teased Rozen. "Well, I'm going in." She swished into the darkness, leaving Zethar floating alone outside.

"Roz! Come out!" hissed Zethar. But she could neither see nor hear her friend. *How far had she gone?* Even though she wasn't within the cave itself, Zethar felt a rise of fear at being left alone, and steeling herself, she swam in after Rozen.

The water inside felt colder and stale, as if never stirred by currents. She couldn't see anything ahead of her, and a few metres in she stopped and called for Rozen again. No answer came. Zethar was about to turn and flee from the cave when a swift shape suddenly knocked her aside. She yelped, terrified, then realised the spectre was only Rozen, who had been lurking against the wall and had shot out past her.

"Oh, that's not funny!" she shouted at her giggling friend, who now floated just outside the cave entrance. "I thought you were a shark, or... what's happening?"

The view of the lighted exterior diminished, suddenly blocked off. Zethar tried to rush out but a strong swirl of water washed her back. Then there was no light, and she was left in total blackness.

"Rozen! Help!" she screamed. But she could not hear her friend, just a rumbling that gradually decreased to silence.

Horrific realisation came to the young maid. The ceiling of the cave, disturbed by their activity, had done what the clan had once feared it would. It had collapsed, sealing her in. She was completely trapped.

For a moment she panicked, swirling round in the black water until dizziness overcame her. Then she tried to calm herself. *These used to be air caves, so there must be other chambers deeper within. Maybe there were other passages leading out too.*

But this hope was soon extinguished. She had no light. The phosphorescent organisms illuminating the inhabited caves were brought up from deeper water by the fishers, especially for the purpose. None had been brought here in years, and although mermaid's eyes coped well in low light, they needed at least some to see. She could not find her way through the passages, as she now had no idea which way she was even facing. Feeling the walls didn't help. They were too irregular. She could easily miss a small opening that might lead the right way.

With no prospect but to wait here until she could no longer hold her breath and then to drown in the darkness, Zethar sat hunched on the cave floor and began to sing to herself for comfort. She sang the melody her mother had sung to her for as long as she could remember, the lullaby that sent her to sleep as a baby. She always hummed it to herself when she was upset, to recall feelings of safety and comfort. And now, in this dire situation, that was what she did.

Her eyes were closed as she sang, her voice unsteady, the notes trembling. They resonated through the small space, which lent a reverberation to her voice.

And as she sang, she saw a spark in the darkness.

A small glimmer, like a glowing worm, spun past the corner of her eye. She stopped singing and looked around, her eyes wide open now but seeing nothing. *Surely my eyes were closed while I sang? Did I imagine the light?* Unsure, she began the song again.

Once again, a flicker, and then another. Yes, her eyes had definitely been closed. What was it? Could it be the ghosts of the folk who had died in this terrible place, come to assist her into the next world? She continued to sing, clinging to her only means of comfort. When the glint came again, she did not stop.

And the flickers continued, like spectral lines and sparks in the darkness. And still she sang, louder now, as if it would make these terrible visions fade. Whether her eyes were open or closed made no difference, still the lights appeared before her, pulsing almost in synchrony with her song.

And then she realised the mysterious illumination was outlining the walls of the cave for her. She could *see!*

Overjoyed, she turned about her, examining her surroundings. As she did so, she stopped her song and all became black again.

The ghosts want me to sing for them! They will show me the way out if I do.

Resuming the song, the granular image returned. Quickly, she cast about her. *There!* She saw a passage she had not noticed before, leading upwards, and swam eagerly towards it. She would need to take a breath soon, and there was no time to tarry.

The passage soon turned level and then twisted left and right, wide enough for three to swim abreast. Zethar sang as if her life depended on it—which seemed to be the case. She no longer felt so scared, just determined and concentrating on interpreting the unreal vision she was experiencing, to spot turnings that might lead out of the passage. She came across one and swam down it, only to find it led to a blind chamber with no air. Retracing her route to the main passage, she carried on as fast as she dared, her lungs now feeling the ache of her need for oxygen. She could only hold for another two minutes, at most.

The passage opened out into a wide chamber, and the strange flickering image did not show her as far as the back of this vast space. This would have been where the clan had lived and slept, and they would have had air in here. So up she swam, charging towards the ceiling, her chest aching more than ever.

There might be a bubble still up there...

But no. She saw the flickering edges of a hard rock ceiling above her, no trace of air at all. Her singing faltered, and so did the image. She kept humming, knowing it was speeding her need for air, but utterly dependent on the music for her life. And there it was—another passage leading upwards.

She threw herself towards it, moving ever higher to where air might be. It was a narrow passage, and she could feel the walls on either side. Unable to sing any more, her visual image faded away. She began to feel dizzy and groped with her hands to continue.

And then ahead of her, the faint glow of light. Real light.

She flung herself forward with all her strength, squeezing her slim body through the rocky tube, which had only just enough width to allow her through. And just as her reflexes tried to force her to gasp, whether she was still underwater or not, her head cleared the surface and sweet air surrounded her.

She had never breathed so deeply in her life.

Zethar did not notice nor care where she was, only that she could breathe, and she was out of the dreadful cave complex. She crawled up and flopped over on her back on the wet rocks, stretching out and relishing freedom. Only then did she look about her. She was in another cave, but one above the waterline. The passage she had come up through led down under what looked like a shallow pool when observed from the surface. At low tide, air could flow freely down the passage into the large cavern. The water level was only about half a metre deep within this cave, and land-folk could easily wade in. Having recovered her energy, Zethar made her way to the entrance and peeped out. Beyond the cave lay a tiny inlet that would only have presented a dry surface at low tide. She swam out beyond this and dived down to return to the village.

****

When she reached home, her mother's face revealed her worry.

"Thank goodness you're safe!" she cried, hugging her daughter tightly. "Rozen came to the fields to find me. She said you were trapped. Is that right?"

"Yes, Mother. We went into the old air caves, and the rocks fell and blocked the entrance before I could get out.

I managed to find a passage leading up to the surface."

"Well, we had better get back along there quickly. Rozen has led some of the men there to try and dig you out."

They swiftly sped through the water to the site of the rock fall. Five mermen were doing their best to heave the rocks out of the entrance, while Rozen circled above, her tail fin tight with worry.

"It's all right," called Morveren as they came near, "Zethar found a way out!"

The men cheered and rushed over to the pair, and Rozen joined them, looking extremely relieved.

"Oh Zethi, I thought I'd never see you again," she said. "How did you find a way out? Was there air in there? And it was so dark, and..."

"Hush, Rozen. Let's go back home and let Zethar calm herself a while, then she can tell us all about it," said Morveren.

The party made their way back to the village plateau. Now Kerra and Kensa joined their sister, bringing her some mackerel in case she was hungry. Zethar's stomach growled on seeing the food. The ordeal had left her drained of energy and she welcomed the fish. The men went to spread the word that the girl was safely home, while the maids sat in an open sandy area and urged Zethar to tell her story.

"It was very scary," she said, in between mouthfuls of mackerel. "I went in after Rozen, because I was worried."

"I didn't mean for you to get stuck!" protested her friend. "I didn't realise it wasn't safe."

"Senara had told you why we abandoned those caves though, hadn't she?" said Morveren, her voice stern. Rozen looked sheepish and fell silent.

Zethar continued her tale. "The rocks fell, and I couldn't get out. It was so dark. I couldn't see anything at all—completely black. And I knew I would need air soon, too."

"It sounds awful!" said Kerra.

"I was terrified," admitted her sister. "I didn't know what to do. So I sat down and sang to myself to try and keep calm. And then the strangest thing happened. The ghosts of the people who died in the cave heard the song and lit the way for me."

The girls looked astonished at this, and Morveren seemed taken aback.

"How do you mean, they lit the way?" she asked.

"It was a sort of strange light, not like any I've seen before," said Zethar. "It appeared only when I sang—a little at first, like small flashes, then more of them, until I could see where the walls were in the darkness, even with my eyes shut."

"Did you see the ghosts themselves?" asked Rozen eagerly.

"No... Just the light they cast for me. They must have been friendly ghosts. I found a passage leading to a wide chamber, and in the roof was a tunnel leading up to a beach cave. I got out just in time. I thought I would die if I went another second without air. If the ghosts hadn't helped me, I would surely have drowned."

"I'm sorry I made you go in there," said Rozen, laying her head on Zethar's shoulder. "I was only playing a game."

"I know, Roz. It's not your fault." Zethar consoled her friend.

"And Senara will be cross with me. I forgot to bring the bag of clams back too."

****

As it turned out, when they saw her the following day, Senara wasn't angry, just relieved neither of them had come to any real harm. She gave Rozen a mild scolding, realising the young maid had been foolish rather than malicious and could not have known how dangerous the situation was. She was intensely curious about Zethar's experience.

"So these lights came when you began to sing. Is that right?" asked Senara. Zethar nodded.

"Yes. Whenever I stopped, I was left in darkness. So I didn't stop, even though I was going to need air very soon."

"Hmm..." Senara stroked her chin, deep in thought. "I want to try something. Come with me, you two."

The wise one led her students to the nearest part of the Shelf, where the coastal shallows descended into deeper water. Here the hunters patrolled, defending against incoming sharks and spearing large fish wandering in from the vast Atlantic beyond. They descended a short way down the side of the Shelf. Zethar felt a flutter of nervousness. They were warned not to go beyond the edge without one of the hunters to guard them, but she would be safe with the wise one. They descended only a little then stopped in front of a recess in the rock, too shallow to be called a proper cave. Senara turned to Zethar.

"I want you to try something for me. First, face away from me, out towards the water."

Zethar did as instructed and Senara seemed to approve. *What is all this about?*

"Now, I want you to close your eyes, and sing your song again, the one you sang when you were trapped. Try and do it exactly as you did before."

Feeling puzzled and self-conscious, Zethar began to hum gently.

"That's lovely," she heard Senara say. "Can you make it a fraction louder, please?"

Zethar raised her volume, still utterly confused as to the purpose of the exercise. Senara touched her arm and indicated for her to stop and open her eyes again.

"So tell me," said the wise one, "did you see any lights at all, like you did in the cave?"

"No... But there are no ghosts here, are there?"

Senara chuckled. "No, not here. There's nothing unusual at all. Now, just come here and face into the entrance of this nook, if you please."

Rozen looked startled. "It's not going to fall in and trap her, is it?" she asked, her voice quavering with anxiety.

"Really, Rozen, do you think I'd subject Zethar to something like that all over again? I assure you it's safe. Now Zethar, if you could close your eyes, and begin the song again, just like before..."

Zethar hummed the notes, the same as she had done a minute earlier, her eyes tight shut. And there it was again—a spark on her peripheral vision, then another, then a faint outline around the interior of the cavity, and even with her eyes shut, she could see the twinkling image. She broke off the song abruptly and opened her eyes, astonished.

"Senara! I can... I can see it again! The lights are back, just like before! Are the ghosts still here?"

Rozen shrank back behind her mentor at the suggestion of ghostly presences, but Senara laughed and took Zethar's hand.

"Oh no, my dear, not at all. And it wasn't ghosts who gave you sight in the dark before. It was you yourself!"

"What do you mean?" asked the bewildered maid.

"Let's go back up and I'll explain," said Senara. She led them up to the safer ground behind the Shelf, and they sat together on the rocky sea bed. The wise one began her explanation.

"There is a legend among our people. Have you heard of the Song of the Dolphin?"

The two girls shook their heads. Senara continued.

"It is said that—very rarely—a maid is born who has a talent for seeing without sight. As dolphins and whales can see by singing, so it is rumoured a maid may have this skill too. It cannot be learned; it is a natural gift that is with you from birth but not always noticed at first. I have never, in all my years, met a maid who had this talent, until now. I couldn't quite believe you might have it, Zethar, until my test just now proved it to me. The water is invisible to the Song, but an enclosed space or hard rocky wall will return an image, in the same way light itself can shine off an object when illuminated. You are using sound in place of light, with quite spectacular results."

Zethar found it hard to wrap her head around this concept. Could she see through her ear holes? What did it all mean? Rozen's mouth hung open, and she stared at Zethar as if her friend had indeed turned into a dolphin.

"But why does it happen? What is it for?" asked Zethar. Senara shrugged.

"Who can say, my dear? It is what it is—a gift of which only you may know the purpose. And maybe not for many years yet. I suggest you don't shy away from it. Don't fear it—but instead explore this talent, practice it, understand how it works, and how it may be put to use."

They swam back to Senara's home to continue the day's tuition, though little was learned, as both Zethar and Rozen were too full of questions and excitement about this seemingly magical skill. Senara didn't know all the answers but tried to reassure the girls that the power was to be welcomed as a blessing. When teaching was done for the day, the wise one accompanied the girls back to the air caves in order to speak to Morveren about her daughter's gift.

"The Song of the Dolphin? My Zethar... really?" Morveren's eyes were wide with disbelief. "I have heard tell of the ability, yes... but I thought it merely a tale of legend."

"It's true," confirmed Senara, "I can find no other explanation. Test her if you wish. Place a blindfold over her eyes and when she sings, she will still be able to find her way within the cave."

"Ooh, let's make her do it!" Kerra jiggled up and down. "I want to see this!"

"Hush, dearest," chided Morveren. "Your sister was

not given this for your entertainment. It is a power to be respected, not paraded for our amusement."

But Zethar was eager to test it for herself, and by the time she had been blindfolded and was ready to go, a small crowd of onlookers had gathered. Kerra spun her sister around three times and pointed her across the cave.

"Off you go, Zethi!" she cried, giving her an unnecessary slap on the tail.

Zethar began to hum, at first not quite loudly enough to get a clear image. The kelp blindfold fitted well enough that no light could reach her eyes, but as she increased the volume of her song, so patterns became clear to her and she cruised easily through the water with no risk of bumping the sides. She could even see the other maids and men in the water, although not well enough to recognise who was who. When she had weaved around the main chamber twice, gone down a side passage and back, and descended to the cave floor without so much as brushing the walls, she returned to her audience and pulled off the blindfold.

The clamour of acclamation and delight from the clan echoed loud in the chamber, and a feeling of pride warmed her. She was special; she had something nobody else in the clan did, and she had never experienced that before. As the youngest of four daughters, she didn't yet have the strength and beauty of Tamon and Kensa. She was not as quick fingered and creative as Kerra, and she had always felt Rozen was better at mixing medicines than she was. But now she had her own unique gift, and nothing else mattered.

"I knew I was right to take her as my second acolyte," murmured Senara to Morveren. "It is a sign she has a destiny ahead of her."

"That's good, isn't it?" asked Morveren. The old mermaid paused before replying.

"I hope so."

CHAPTER THREE
Tales from Other Places

Over the next few months, Zethar attempted to refine and understand her talent. She soon learned the images she saw were dependent on the pitch of the notes she sang—higher notes gave more clarity and detail, while lower ones passed farther through the water and increased her field of vision. Materials also appeared differently in the sound-pictures—rock showed a clear image, mud and sand were less distinct, and seaweed remained virtually invisible for some reason.

But the most startling aspect of the phenomenon was what the young maid saw when she looked at living creatures. Hard-shelled crustaceans and molluscs gave an image similar to that of stone, which made sense to her. They were of similar texture. But when she looked closely at fish and at her fellow merfolk, the vision was different. From a distance, their skin showed clearly, delineating the outline of tails, arms, and heads. But the closer she came to them, the more she saw what lay beneath the skin—muscles, organs, and then the reflections of the bones themselves.

At first this scared her, but then she forgot her fear and became fascinated with it. Merfolk had only a rudimentary knowledge of their own anatomy, so by the time Zethar turned twelve, her knowledge of the internal layout of her people surpassed even Senara's.

She still continued her studies alongside Rozen, but she had noticed a change in the attitude of the girl who had been her best friend. Rozen no longer seemed so caring and friendly to Zethar, tending to spend her social time with some of the other girls rather than her fellow acolyte as she had before. None of Zethar's other friends showed any resentment towards her since she discovered her talent, and she realised the reason for Rozen's withdrawal. They had been equals as acolytes, neither ahead of the other. But then Rozen was left behind. Everyone marvelled at Zethar's amazing gift; everyone talked about how special she was. Nobody said there was anything special about Rozen.

Zethar attempted to prevent the rift between them growing wider, kept trying to explain that she really was just the same as she always had been, and there were many things Rozen could do better than her. But the other girl seemed only to sulk more, and the continued praise of Zethar by the rest of the clan didn't help matters.

* * * *

As the months became years, so Senara came to rely on her pupils more and more to carry out her daily duties. Her arms became stiff with age and travelling around the broad area occupied by the clan tired her. Nobody was sure how old she was, but certainly older than everyone else. One day, when she was sixteen, Zethar's curiosity led her to ask Senara about her early life. The pair were tending plants in the shallows when Zethar chose her moment.

"Senara... were you born here? Or did you come from elsewhere?"

The elderly maid raised her eyebrows in surprise, pausing in her work.

"That's not something I get asked much, you know. As it happens, I am from another clan, away to the northwest—from the west coast of what the land-folk call Ireland."

Zethar had heard of this place, but she had never left her local waters. "So how did you come to be with us... if you don't mind me asking?"

Senara smiled, reassuring the girl she was not impertinent.

"Many years ago, when I was a similar age to yourself, I studied the craft just as you do now. But I was a careless girl and didn't concentrate as much as I should. One day I had been asked to mix some medicine for two sick children, twin sisters, who were only four years old. They had tail blight—and I'm sure you know the remedy for that, don't you?" Senara fixed her acolyte with a beady eye, and Zethar racked her brain to give the right answer to this impromptu test.

"Umm... a mixture of puffer fish extract, ground cuttle bone, and fermented kelp stem?" she said, hoping her list was correct.

Senara nodded her approval. "You have been paying more attention than I did, I see. Well, I prepared the mixture as my mistress asked me to—except I forgot to add in the cuttle bone. Without it, the medicine is not only useless for treating the blight, but it becomes actively poisonous. And without realising what I had made, I took the brew to the children and administered it."

It shocked Zethar to hear this confession coming from the woman she viewed as infallible, wise and perfect in judgement.

"You can imagine what happened," Senara said. "Within an hour of taking the mixture, they both became very ill indeed. They suffered stomach cramps and sickness, and became dizzy and delirious. The following day, one of them died." Senara hung her head, her expression sadder than Zethar had ever seen. "The other survived, recovering after a few days, but the damage was done. I had killed one of my own clan."

"But it was an accident, wasn't it?" Zethar protested. "You didn't mean for that to happen."

Senara nodded. "Oh yes, it was an accident. Everyone accepted that. Nobody thought I had done it on purpose, but still the error was mine and I took responsibility. My mistress told me my training must stop, and I was no longer destined to be a wise one after she had gone."

"But you *are* now. Did she change her mind?"

Senara shook her head slowly, her white hair drifting in the current.

"No. From that day, the rest of the clan looked down upon me. People were polite to my face, but behind my back they spoke dark words and wouldn't trust me with anything. The child's parents never forgave me, of course. And with my goal lost, without the hope of ever completing the path to wisdom, I felt I had no reason to live any more. There was no comfort in my home, so I left."

"Where did you go?" Zethar's curiosity increased.

"I had no destination in mind. I just wanted to leave the terrible thing I had done far behind and I set out to the south, passing round the far reaches of Ireland until I came to the Atlantic. Heading west would take me only to deeper and more dangerous seas, so I turned east, towards the waters we call Candtowan. The land-folk call it Cardigan Bay. I knew not what I would find."

"And what did you find?"

"I found my destiny was not to be cast aside after all, merely diverted to a more complex path." Senara smiled at Zethar's puzzlement. "I found another clan of maids there, very different to the one I had known, and very different to ours too."

The young maid wondered what she meant. "How

were they different?"

"Unlike our group—and the one I had come from—their society was less... organised, I suppose. We all have our roles—farmer, craftsmaid, and so on. But they all did some of everything. Obviously each had different aptitudes, as we do, but knowledge and skills were shared among them and all carried out multiple tasks to varying degrees. To them, the position of wise one was not a single role, but one in which they all shared some skill."

This struck Zethar as an extremely odd way of living. *How would one know what to do on any given day?*

Senara must have sensed her scepticism. "I know it sounds strange," she said, "but it worked for them."

She stopped and looked about her. Zethar realised the tide was going out and they had to return to deeper water. She popped her head up to breathe then plunged down, and the two of them swam back towards home. Senara continued her story as they went.

"The Candtowan clan took me in and made me welcome, not questioning my reason for coming. From them I continued to learn the arts of healing, divination, and midwifery. I'm sure you won't believe it looking at my frail body now, but I also became something of a hunter!"

Zethar indeed found it hard to picture her mentor as a strong, young maid with a hunter's spear, and smiled at the mental image she created.

"So why did you leave them and come to our clan?"

"After five years with them, there came a problem. The land folk had begun to fish in our home area, using deep nets that trawled the very sea bed. One maid was killed by entanglement in such a net, and the leader of the clan decided a new territory must be found. Several of us dispersed to look for suitable areas, and I travelled south to the waters of Kernow to see what was there."

"And that's when you found our clan!"

Senara nodded. "Yes. I took such a liking to the place and the people that I never went back. I sometimes wonder if I should have returned, but I felt I belonged here. I sometimes think about the Candtowan clan and hope they found a safe place to live. I should have told them about this place, but..." She paused, looking down at the sand. "I don't know if they even exist anymore." The old maid's voice held a note of regret.

"Well, I'm glad you stayed with us. I don't know what we'd do without you," said Zethar.

"That's as may be, but *I* know exactly what they would do. They would manage fine with you and Rozen to guide them."

Zethar flushed with pride at Senara's words. They had reached Senara's weed store and carefully stowed away the plants they had collected. Rozen appeared a few minutes later with some delicate jellyfish in a fine net.

"An excellent catch, Rozen. It must have taken some time to find all those," said the wise one.

"It did. They're hard to see. Though I expect Zethar could have squawked at them and they'd light up for her."

The sarcasm hurt Zethar. She had done nothing to annoy Rozen today and besides, what she said wasn't even accurate. Jellyfish were largely invisible to her sound vision. She debated whether or not to say so but held her tongue, not wishing an argument to break out.

Senara changed the subject. "Thank you both for your assistance. I think we're done for the day. Oh, let me give you some of these," she said to Zethar, handing her some slender sea grass stems from her pouch. "Your sister has a use for them, I believe."

The acolytes headed home, not speaking to each other.

****

"Oh Zethi, those are perfect!"

Kerra's eyes lit with delight on seeing the thin strips of weed her sister had brought her.

"Whatever do you need them for? Your jewellery?"

Zethar queried. Kerra nodded, examining the stems.

"Yes. To make special bracelets." Although her main duty was farming sea lettuce, Kerra had become an accomplished jewellery maker in her spare time. Zethar's own exquisite necklace of small stones and shells was her handiwork.

"So why can't you just go and get your own sea grass, rather than depleting Senara's stock?"

Kerra's smile was mischievous. "Because Senara has blessed these stems. So when they are made into a bracelet and it's given to a land-man..."

"Then if he puts it on, he will fall in love with you forever," finished Zethar. "Of course. But you don't have a land-man to give it to, do you?"

"No, but I don't just make these for myself. Kensa wants to have one ready, in case she meets someone, and Lusanda and Tressa are on the lookout too. There's a lot of demand, you know. Are you able to do the blessing ritual yourself yet? That would be easiest. Then I could just get you to make the grass magic for me."

Zethar rolled her eyes. "Yes, but it's not that simple. The blessing has to be done when the moon is in the right shape, and—"

A shout from outside the cave interrupted her. Ciaran, one of the merman hunters, darted into the entrance.

"Stay inside!" he commanded.

"What's going on?" asked Kerra, peering out cautiously.

Ciaran's face was grim.

"Shark attack."

CHAPTER FOUR
Shark and Swordfish

The mermaid village extended from the coastal cliffs out to the Shelf, where the sea floor dropped away to dark depths. Beyond lay the Atlantic, thousands of miles of open ocean where few merfolk ever ventured. But the denizens of the ocean realm sometimes made their way into shallower water and occasionally dangerous creatures were among them.

"Ciaran, what happened?" Zethar asked, hoping nobody had been hurt.

The muscular hunter stowed his spear and came further into the cave to explain. "Raoul was fishing a short distance from the Shelf. A shark came in from below—an isur."

The maid's tails folded in fear. Isurs, as the merfolk called them, were one of the fastest and most dangerous species of shark. They could not be out-swum, and engaging one in combat was a dangerous risk. Though rarely encountered, they had a taste for merflesh and would attack without provocation.

"Is Raoul all right?" asked Kerra. The fisherman was a well-liked member of the clan who had an unusual history.

Rather than coming from the land nearby to join the merfolk, Raoul hailed from the warm lands of the Mediterranean. His maidwife had died shortly after she had taken him as a husband, and he had left his home waters in search of new companionship—and he'd found it. He and Rozen had become close since his arrival a year ago, although he was older than her.

Ciaran shook his head. "He has been bitten. How badly, I do not know. The shark disappeared back over the edge of the Shelf and Raoul sank down with it. Your sister Tamon has gone in pursuit... no other of us dared swim after it." Ciaran looked somewhat ashamed, but Zethar was hit by a pang of worry for her brave sister. Tamon was a capable hunter, but to take on an isur was more foolish than courageous. Yet she also admired her sister's daring, when all the other hunters had held back.

"Zethi, don't even think about it," warned Kerra, having noticed her sister drifting closer to the mouth of the cave. "I've already got two sisters in danger out there. Remember, we don't know where Kensa is—or Mother." The elder twin was probably working the kelp fields with Morveren, but whether the shark would come close to those regions was impossible to say. If it did, the only cover was the long fronds of the giant algae. There was nowhere entirely safe they could reach.

More people were entering the cave now, speeding in from wherever they had been, out in the open sea. Zethar kept an eye out for any of her family and was relieved to see Morveren and Kensa dart in. They were not aware of what had happened, only that there was a shark warning. Morveren visibly blanched when she heard Tamon had pursued the beast. The girls tried their best to reassure her, but they too were desperately worried. The occupants of the cave counted heads. Some maids had been seen going to ground in Senara's refuge, so their whereabouts was known, but eventually there were only two missing—Tamon and Raoul.

The clan waited, an anxious murmur passing among them. Ciaran kept peeking out to see if there was a sign of either the missing pair or the shark and every time he came back in, Zethar's heart leapt, hoping to hear news. But there was none.

Then after twenty minutes, Ciaran shouted, "They're coming!"

In through the entrance swept Tamon, carrying the injured and unconscious Raoul in her arms. Blood trailed from puncture wounds on his back and Rozen cried out and rushed forward to him. Tamon carried him through to one of the smaller side chambers where he could be placed on a supporting ledge. Rozen followed closely, her tail clenching with distress, and Zethar went with them to assist.

"The shark is dead," announced Tamon and reaching behind her back, she drew a dark triangular object from her harness—the shark's dorsal fin, sliced off as a trophy. But the triumph was muted. The hunter looked down at the man she had rescued.

"We're going to need Senara. His wounds will not be easy to heal."

She flipped around and powered out of the cave to fetch the wise one. Meanwhile, Zethar examined Raoul closely, while Rozen did not do much more than flit and sob around them, forgetting her training. Her flustering could be forgiven with the way she felt about the handsome merman.

He had been gripped in the shark's jaws, and its multiple rows of teeth had made a pattern of small tears in his skin on both front and back. His back continued to bleed the worst, emerging rivulets appearing black in the dim blue light. Zethar assessed the injury; they would need to bind around these wounds to prevent further blood loss. She asked one of the other maids to fetch her some broad kelp leaves, which would serve as ideal bandages.

"He can't die! Oh Raoul, wake up!" said Rozen,

stroking his face. The merman stirred briefly but then again became unresponsive.

"Rozen, I need you to help me," said Zethar, trying to snap her out of her frantic state. "He will need ointment for his skin to heal the cuts. Can you make some?"

"Yes, yes, of course. I'll do that," said Rozen and after dithering for a moment, she left her sweetheart's side and went to prepare the medicine. Zethar could concentrate better without the distraction. Before long, Tamon returned with Senara, who carried her large medicine pouch. She narrowed her eyes as she saw the damage inflicted by the isur.

"This is a serious injury. Do you have ointment for the skin?"

"Yes," replied Zethar. "Rozen is preparing it. She should be back any minute. I was going to bind him with kelp leaves."

Senara nodded her approval. "Yes, that's exactly right. But we need more than medicine to complete his healing. I must pray for a blessing."

Raoul was propped up so his torso was out of the water, resting on the rocky ledge inside the cave's air bubble. Senara slithered up onto the ledge, right out of the water, and cradled his head on her lap. Placing her hands on his temples, she began a gentle chant. Soon after, Rozen returned with a shell full of a creamy paste. She and Zethar applied the balm to Raoul's body and then sealed it in under the kelp bandages. Senara came to the end of her mantra and they carefully lowered the merman down into the water. As his head submerged, he opened his eyes.

"Rozen! What happened... how am I still alive?" He winced as the girl flung her arms around him. "I remember the shark had me in its mouth, then I saw Tamon coming, and that's all I know."

Tamon explained what had happened to him, and Raoul thanked the wise one and her acolytes for tending to him. But he still looked pale and movement hurt him a great deal.

"Now you must rest, my lad. Stay with Rozen and don't do any fishing for at least another week," Senara advised.

With Raoul fixed up, the next task was to retrieve the body of the shark. Tamon and a couple of her fellow hunters left the cave to collect it. There would be a fine feast made of its flesh tonight.

****

The following morning, Zethar went to check on Raoul. He'd stayed with Rozen at the back of the large sleeping cave, and it shocked her to see he looked far worse than he had the day before. His eyes were closed and his pale face and chest were blotchy. The skin of his tail fin was a sickly purple colour.

"He's fine," protested Rozen. "He just didn't sleep well."

"He's clearly not fine. Something is going on inside him. And we need to know what."

"Oh no, you don't! No staring into my man!" Rozen had guessed Zethar's intentions.

Zethar sighed. "Look, Roz, it's the only way we will know if he's hurt deeper inside."

"I want her to do it." Raoul said, his eyes opening.

"Well, that settles it," said Zethar. She bent down and placed her forehead gently against Raoul's waist, while Rozen retreated to a distance with a sour expression. Zethar began to hum a single note, high and clear, and closed her eyes.

The image came into focus. The bright reflections of Raoul's ribs were all she could see at first, but she adjusted her voice's pitch and her head position until she could see beyond them, into the abdominal cavity. There! A large vessel pulsed, carrying blood down to his lower organs and tail. Zethar pressed close against Raoul's body, trying to see as clearly as she could. She should be able to see the bright bone at the other side of the merman's pelvis, but something was fuzzy in front of it, a mass of something standing in the way. She stopped her song and pulled back, looking up at Raoul.

"You're bleeding inside. It's leaking from one of your blood tubes."

Rozen put her hand to her face, worried. "Are you sure? Do you know for certain?"

"I'm pretty sure. I think we will need cailplena in the strongest dose and something for the pain."

"Yes. Minnarin and a dash of urchin extract?" suggested Rozen. Zethar nodded.

"We'll have you feeling better soon," she said to her patient.

Raoul gave a weak nod then his eyes closed again. Rozen nestled against him, stroking his hair.

****

"Zethi! Did you hear the news!" Tamon was grinning as she approached her sister.

"I don't think so, what is it?" Zethar had been helping Raoul for the last couple of hours and had not heard any gossip. The merman had been given his medicine to stop the internal bleeding; only time would tell if the cure worked.

"I'm to be given the status of Swordfish," said Tamon.

"Oh! That's marvellous. I'm so happy for you!" exclaimed Zethar. The title of Swordfish was awarded to hunters who had excelled with brave deeds, and it was a rare honour. There would be a ceremony held on shore at the next full moon to award it.

"I'm going to the fields to tell Kensa and Mother. Kerra already knows. See you later!" She sped off, her copper hair streaming behind her. Zethar returned to the cave to continue helping Rozen and found Senara had come to check on him too.

"I just heard Tamon's to become a Swordfish," she told the wise one, who smiled and nodded.

"Yes, I was among those who nominated her. She did an immensely brave thing, and she thoroughly deserves the reward. The next full moon is in three days, so we will hold the ceremony then, at the cove. I think it would be a good opportunity for one of you two to do the tattooing."

Mermaids of exceptional prowess in their skill often bore blessed tattoos to mark their status, and the accolade of Swordfish was one of these. Zethar knew Senara held tattooing to be a deeply serious matter, and frowned on the recent practice among younger maids of being tattooed simply for decoration; she thought it demeaning to the sacred art. To allow one of her acolytes to perform that part of the ceremony was a mark of high trust in them.

"I think Zethar ought to," said Rozen, quite surprising her. "I don't have an eye for art like she does, and I don't think I have a steady enough hand. Tamon is more likely to forgive her own sister if she makes a mistake."

Although the last part was rather insulting, Zethar had to agree, and was pleased to get the chance.

"Well then, that's sorted out," said Senara. "Rozen, you can prepare the ink for her. Now, I think my acolytes have done all they can for you, Raoul. Continue to rest and you will be fine."

Senara left, and Rozen went with her to discuss the details of making the ink, leaving Raoul and Zethar alone.

"I owe my life to Tamon. She is a wonderful Swordfish," he said. "But also, I owe it to you. Senara told me that without your Dolphin Song, I might not have survived."

Zethar blushed. "It was nothing. It's what I do. Anyone else would do it if they could. It's not like it's a choice, or—"

She stopped, startled, as Raoul bent his head to kiss her gently on the lips. He slipped his arm around her waist, and gave her back a gentle stroke. Zethar was too surprised to do anything but sit immobile on the rocky ledge. Then without a word, she flipped off into the water and made a hasty exit. She heard him call after her, but she didn't look back.

****

"Uh, really? He actually *kissed* you?" Tamon cocked her head, brows knitted. The pair sat in the sunshine on one of the wide, flat rocks at the beach the land-folk called Trelanton Cove, where the forthcoming Swordfish ceremony would take place.

"Yes. He kissed me." Zethar confirmed. "He was... well, he was just grateful for my part in helping him. That's all it was."

"No. That's not how you express gratitude to someone. Maybe to Rozen, of course, but to you... that can't have been a simple 'thank you' gesture."

Zethar's recollection of the man's soft caress along her back told her Tamon was quite correct. She sighed.

"I'm not interested, anyway. I shall find my own husband one day. I'm not going to steal my friend's man."

"Of course. Now... remind me, how do I have to lie when you mark me?"

The planning of the ceremony continued, and no more was said about the kiss.

****

The blow took Zethar entirely by surprise when it came. She hadn't even known Rozen was there waiting for her.

"Oww! What are you doing?" Zethar rubbed her stinging cheek where her one-time friend had landed a punch. They were beneath a rocky outcrop on the route from the beach to the air caves.

"You traitor!" screeched Rozen. "Tressa told me. She

was picking winkles among the rock pools. She heard everything you said to Tamon!"

"But I didn't do anything," Zethar began to protest. Rozen wasn't in a mood to listen.

"Didn't *do* anything? You *kissed* him!" she hissed, moving in uncomfortably close.

"I did not! He kissed me. I was just sitting there and he bent down and— "

"Liar!" shouted Rozen. "You knew he was mine, and you couldn't wait to take him away from me too." She circled Zethar, tail thrashing the water angrily. "First it was your precious Song of the Dolphin. Everyone forgot Senara had another acolyte. They only saw you, because you're so magical and special. Isn't Zethar wonderful, with her amazing skill nobody has ever seen before? Haven't the gods blessed her? Poor Rozen. She's too ordinary now. Nobody thinks of her as a wise one. She's just there as a backup."

Zethar was shocked to hear these words. She hadn't realised Rozen had harboured such deep resentment for so long.

"Roz, I never meant it to be that way. I don't want to be thought of as any more special than you,"

"Nonsense. You enjoy being the perfect one. And when you had the chance to be perfect and make a move on my sweet Raoul at the same time, you couldn't resist."

"*He* made the move! He leant in and kissed me. Ask Tamon if you don't believe me. She knows the full story," protested Zethar.

"Oh, like your sister isn't going to side with you? Raoul would never favour you. He loves me—and *only* me." She tossed her head, her blonde hair rippling in the current.

"I've told you what happened. If you choose not to believe it, then fine. Talk to Raoul. I don't care what you think."

Zethar let her tears flow free as she swam the rest of the way to the cave.

In the days that followed, Rozen refused to talk to Zethar, though she did try to make peace. Sometimes they inevitably had to be in the same place when studying and working under Senara's instruction, but the atmosphere was always tense. As for Raoul, he no longer appeared to hold any affection for Rozen—they had been observed arguing—and he actively avoided Zethar too.

Even with the passage of months, the coldness between the two maids did not thaw.

CHAPTER FIVE
Accusations

One fine evening, when the crescent moon decorated the evening sky and the tide was still strong, Senara summoned her pupils to a meeting above the surface. The three of them bobbed in the water, not far from the shore.

"I am not as young as I wish I still was," said the wise one. "I have served this clan for fifty years, seen countless maids come and go, and even more men pass their brief lives with us. Every maid with us now I have known from a baby. And now there is a tiredness upon me."

Zethar knew there was truth in the elderly maid's words. She had noticed Senara becoming less active of late—finding difficulty in swimming longer distances, not being able to hold her breath as long as she could before, and needing more hours of sleep.

"I have taught you both the arts of healing and the sacred rituals of our people. You have exceeded my greatest expectations. The clan will be well provided for in the future, with two as knowledgeable as yourselves. I think it's time I pronounced you ready. There is no more I can teach you. The rest of your path you must take by yourselves."

Zethar was surprised to hear this. For thirteen years she had been accustomed to thinking Senara was infinitely wiser than her. The announcement seemed almost an abrupt end to her tuition.

"We can still assist you though, can't we?" she asked.

Senara smiled.

"Of course. I need you both now more than you need me! The more physically taxing duties are ones I welcome help with."

So they continued to work alongside Senara, but now had less need to be in the same place at the same time, and the pair avoided each other when they could.

****

The following week, Zethar was helping Senara set out a circle on the seabed for a new baby's blessing ceremony. Rozen was away, administering to a maid with an injured eye.

"Senara, do you have the coral branch? I can't find it," said Zethar, rummaging in the pouch the holy items were kept in.

"Yes. It's over... over there," said the wise one. Zethar turned to look, alarmed by the tone of her voice. Senara leaned on the ground, supporting herself with her arms. Something was seriously wrong.

With a flick of her fin, Zethar crossed the circle to the older maid, who looked pale and shaky.

"What's the matter? Do you need air? Let's get you to the surface." Zethar grabbed Senara in her arms and powered upwards, easily carrying her weight. Their heads broke the surface and Senara gasped for air, but she showed no sign of recovering. Zethar had to hold her up in order to stop her from sinking again.

"Zethar, my dear, I don't know what's happening to me. Everything is spinning and my chest hurts. Let me go. I need to lie down."

They swam back to the sea bed, and Senara flopped down in the centre of the circle, clearly in a great deal of pain. Zethar held her shoulders.

"Is there a medicine you need for this? Perhaps rintala? Tell me, please!" said Zethar. But Senara did not respond, just continued to shiver and slump back on the soft sand. Zethar had never seen this condition before. But there was one thing she could try and do.

Placing her forehead against Senara's chest, she steadied her voice and began to hum. The images sparkled into view, but they were of little help. She couldn't see much beyond the ribs, just a dark cloudiness where her sound did not penetrate. The Song did not transmit well through air, and Senara's lungs had enough to frustrate her.

She held the elderly maid close, still trying to tune the pitch to see anything which might be helpful. But then she realised she could no longer feel Senara's heartbeat against her. She pulled back and looked down at the pale face surrounded by the cloud of slowly swaying white hair. Senara had taken the dive into the next world.

Zethar began to cry, but a shout from close by startled her.

"Murderer!"

Rozen floated in the water above them, returned from her duties. She stared down in horror at the scene.

"Rozen, she's dead! Oh, it was awful. She had pain in her chest, and we went up—"

"What did you do? You killed her! I saw you. You put your head to her chest and did your Song, and then the next minute her life left her. Oh, how could you?"

Zethar panicked at this accusation. "I did the Song, yes, but to look into her body and help her! She was already in pain. There was nothing else I could do. Surely you believe me?" But Rozen had already turned, speeding back towards home to deliver the news. Zethar gathered up Senara's body and swam after her, at a slower pace. When she reached the air caves, Rozen had already delivered her version of events. Two hunters slid forward as she approached.

"Rozen accuses you of murder. What has happened?" demanded one.

"I didn't murder Senara! She suffered chest pain and went shaky. I was trying to help," explained the young maid.

"She put her head to her chest and sang the Song of the Dolphin. The next moment Senara was dead," said Rozen loudly. A small crowd had begun to gather to see what the commotion was. Senara's body was taken from her arms and brought into the caves, while the hunters levelled their spears at Zethar.

"What is going on here?" Morveren pushed her way through towards her daughter.

"Mother, Rozen says I killed Senara." Zethar's voice trembled. Morveren tried to move forward to comfort her but the hunters stopped her. Furious, she rounded on Rozen.

"Why would you make such a claim against her? Why would Zethar ever commit such an appalling deed? My daughter is as gentle as any maid in these waters, and murder would be impossible for her."

Rozen held her head high. "Senara had told us we needed no further tuition, as I'm sure Zethar informed you. Where was the advantage in letting Senara live? It's quite clear to me. She was taking the opportunity to raise her status by foul means. She wants to be the only wise one in the clan. I have no doubt that I would have been her next victim."

This suggestion was met with a ripple of murmured consideration by the crowd, which continued to grow. *Surely people would not believe Rozen's outlandish tale?*

"Rozen, this is a very serious accusation," said one of the hunters. Zethar saw her mother sobbing and was glad her three sisters were not present. Knowing Tamon's fierce protective streak, she would likely have taken her blade to Rozen, just for blaming her younger sibling.

"Yes. It's serious, but so was what Zethar did. She must be punished!" cried Rozen.

Morveren spoke up again. "If you wish justice to be done, it must be done properly. No punishment shall be given without a fair hearing of judgement."

The crowd seemed to agree with her on this. The majority of the clan liked Zethar, and she commanded a certain respect from her role as Senara's successor.

"Morveren is right," said the other hunter. "We must form a council of the disciplines and weigh the evidence."

There was rarely a need for trials as such in the society of the merfolk. Most crimes were unknown; murder was extremely rare indeed. There was never any theft, as they had little sense of personal property. When an accusation such as Rozen's was made, a court formed from representatives of six professions was brought into being: one each from the hunters, fishers, crafters, weavers and farmers, plus the clan wise one. However, since the wise one was no longer present in this world and her successors were the accused and accuser, the council would only include the other five professions.

Zethar waited in a small chamber at the back of the air caves while the rest of the clan decided among themselves who would be best to serve the roles on the council. Left alone, she wept, heartbroken as much at the death of her beloved mentor as at the charge against her. She didn't know how much time had passed before a soft hand touched her arm. She looked up into the wide brown eyes of Kensa.

"The members of the council have been decided, Zethi."

"Who?" Zethar both dreaded and hoped to hear who her judges would be. Kensa listed the names. There were those among them who were friendly with Zethar, but also those who were closer to Rozen.

"You know I didn't do it, don't you?" Zethar's small voice quavered. Kensa wrapped her arms around her sister and held her tightly.

"I know. We won't let anything happen to you. Our blood is your blood. We swim with you always."

Zethar slept heavily. Her emotional turmoil had left her exhausted.

****

At dawn the next day, the council convened. Zethar was at liberty to go about her business as she pleased. She found no consolation anywhere, though; her thoughts travelled with her, filling her mind and making her feel sick with unease. Her mother and sisters tried to keep her company, as did her aunt, Delen, but she said she would rather be alone, and they reluctantly let her go her own way. Nobody spoke aloud the dreadful fear they all knew. The traditional penalty for murder was death.

Zethar cruised out to the edge of the Shelf and dived down to the recess where Senara had first helped her understand her rare talent. She sat in there, tail coiled around herself, only moving when she needed to come up for air, then returning.

As the light began to fade towards the end of the day, Zethar left her hiding place and swam back to the village to face whatever judgement had been decided.

In the main chamber, they were waiting for her.

Ciaran, who had represented the hunters on the council, swam forward to deliver the verdict. Around the sides of the chamber, the rest of the clan waited to hear his words.

"We have reached a decision. You may be aware that normally those found guilty of such a terrible crime would meet justice at the end of a spear."

Zethar's heart leapt as fear took hold of her.

"However," Ciaran continued, "This council was

unable to reach a decisive verdict. We could not agree on whether you were guilty. The power Rozen alleges you used is a mystery to the rest of us, and we simply do not know if what she says you did is possible."

Zethar knew Ciaran well enough to know he believed her to be innocent. He wasn't done speaking, though.

"Yet we have to accept you may have had motive, and the circumstances were suspicious. Therefore, we have no alternative but to pass a sentence of lesser severity. You will be exiled from the waters of Kernow. You must go alone, and none may accompany you or seek you out."

She felt faint for a moment. Although her life had been spared, exile was a serious punishment. The merfolk relied on each other's collective skills to survive, to feed and protect each other. On her own, Zethar would find life incredibly difficult.

Then her sisters and mother were by her side, giving hugs and comfort, and she wished she were just a little girl again, no longer the nineteen-year-old maid trained to be wise, but feeling so unknowing and helpless.

"You're still here for tonight, my seagull," Morveren said. "You're still with us."

CHAPTER SIX
The Candtowan

As the sun rose the following morning, Zethar said a tearful goodbye to her family. She took a pouch of food and a knife Tamon had given her for self-defence.

"Where will you go?" asked Kerra.

"I shall head north. Senara once spoke of the clan she used to live with. If they still exist, that is where I may find them."

So Zethar's journey began. Other merfolk were forbidden to follow, and it was a horrible wrench knowing her mother and sisters were watching her swim away until she was lost in the ocean's blue haze. She swam until she reached the edge of the Shelf and kept going, the dark water yawning beneath her to untold depths. She travelled the open sea, with no shelter. Rising up for air, she saw no land about her, but Zethar knew her direction from the position of the sun. She managed to snatch a couple of small fish for sustenance, not wanting to consume her rations unless she had to.

When night fell, she stopped swimming and slept, bobbing at the surface. A risky way to sleep, but she could not go on without rest. When dawn came, bringing with it a light rain, she set off again, moving north and slightly eastwards, always on the lookout for any sign of merfolk or their habitations.

For three days she swam across featureless sea, too deep to detect the bottom. She had eaten her provisions and had to rely on the meagre pickings of fish that came near enough to grab. Twice she came near boats crewed by land-men, not caring if they saw her. She could think of nothing but how she longed for home.

Then, on the morning of the fourth day, she came to shallower water. There was still no land in sight, but a sandy bed dotted with sea grass rose up beneath her. She dived down to inspect it, for such terrain often haboured eels. She was not disappointed. Soon she had caught eight of them and filled her stomach to satisfaction.

But as she sat on the sand, finishing off the last morsel of her breakfast, she sensed a presence. She whirled round to look behind her.

There, just a few metres away, floated another maid. She wore the harness of a hunter and carried a spear, pointed at Zethar. Her pale blonde hair was streaked with brown and framed an angry face.

"Who are you?" Her voice was soft, mismatched to her warlike appearance, with an unusual accent.

"My name is Zethar. I'm... I travelled here from Kernow. I was just having something to eat. I didn't mean to intrude on you." She had never met a maid who was not of her own clan and wasn't sure of the proper way to make an introduction.

The fierce maid looked her up and down. "You carry a weapon. Do you mean harm?"

"No! Not at all. It's for defence."

The maid raised an eyebrow and didn't lower her spear. "I dare say. What brings you here?"

Zethar thought she had better come clean. "I was exiled from my home. I have come looking for the Candtowan clan."

The maid with the streaked hair laughed and placed her spear back in its scabbard on her harness.

"Then welcome, Zethar of Kernow! I am Gwylan of the Candtowan. And while I do not know if you will be permitted to stay in our waters, I can take you to someone who will make that decision. Follow me." Zethar was relieved. At least now she had a chance to find refuge.

Gwylan led Zethar eastward. The water became shallower and before long, Zethar could see land rising on the horizon when she broke the surface. The hunter stayed silent as she swam, and Zethar was apprehensive. *Are the Candtowan all as intimidating as Gwylan?* Then she remembered Senara and her genial nature, and her worry lessened.

They came to a structure the likes of which Zethar had never seen underwater—a great circle, depressed like a crater, around which were columns of varying height, some mere stumps, others a couple of metres tall. They were petrified wood, the trunks of a circle of prehistoric trees, once on land but now swallowed by the water.

Within this circle were many maids going about their business and what appeared to be artificial caves of some kind, with some sort of bizarre coloured hide stretched over unseen supports to make a tent-like dwelling. It astonished Zethar to see it, a scene such as she had never imagined.

They swam down into the centre of the circle, and stopped by a maid with beautiful black hair. She was not dressed as a hunter, but instead wore a finely-crafted circlet of coral on her head, and bracelets of pearly shell.

"Well, who is this? A visitor?" she said as they approached. She spoke with the same accent as Gwylan.

"Speak to her," prompted Gwylan, giving Zethar a small poke.

"Um... hello. I am Zethar. I come in peace," she said, hesitating.

"She was exiled from her own clan," said Gwylan. "I

found her out on the sand banks eating eels. She claims she has come here to find us."

"Exiled? For what… eel theft?" said the black-haired maid. Zethar was afraid for a moment but then noticed a twinkle in her questioner's eye. "It doesn't matter," continued the maid. "If you have come here with the intention to make a fresh start, then whatever you did is of no consequence. We have many among us who have come from elsewhere and found new lives. My name is Rhian, and I am the leader of this clan."

The idea of having one person in charge seemed odd to Zethar, for her own clan had no such figure. She had heard the land-folk also organised their tribes in such a way.

"I hope you may allow me to stay among you," said Zethar, her voice still betraying her nervousness. "I have been trained as a wise one, and I will gladly help you in any way I can."

Rhian's eyes lit up with pleasure on hearing this, and she stretched her tail fin wide. "Excellent to hear. Each clan has skills the others do not know, and your knowledge can be passed on. Here, we will share what we know with you, as you will with us, and we will also teach you other disciplines, should you care to learn them."

This sounded exciting to Zethar. Maybe she could try fishing, or even hunting? Then a thought occurred to her.

"Rhian, there is one skill I possess that is rare among our kind. I have the Song of the Dolphin."

Both Rhian and Gwylan looked surprised and exchanged glances.

"You speak truly?" asked Rhian. "A rare gift indeed. You must be blessed. Can you show us?"

Gwylan set up several stones in an open area of sand and then tied a blindfold over Zethar's eyes. By this time, a host of other curious maids had come to watch the new arrival. Zethar had no difficulty in swimming straight over to each stone and plucking them up from the sea bed with pinpoint accuracy.

"Amazing!" exclaimed Rhian. "You are indeed welcome among the Candtowan, young Zethar."

****

Over the next few days, Zethar got to know the other members of the clan and began to make friends. She discovered Gwylan was not nearly so threatening when she was being sociable, and Rhian seemed lovely in every way. There were few men among the clan at the present time, and no maids currently pregnant, but many of them had a knowledge of midwifery surpassing even Senara's. Zethar learned of new medicines and treatments and in return, she shared her knowledge of anatomy gleaned from her unusual visioning ability.

She became good friends with three maids—Saraid, Tavie and Elizabeth—who had accents quite different from the majority of the clan.

"We are not from these waters originally," explained Tavie. "We come from far to the north, where the sea lochs are home to otters and water horses. Like yourself, we travelled far to get here."

"Your names are unfamiliar to me as well," noted Zethar.

"Ah well, they are common as you like in our seas!" said Saraid. "Except Elizabeth, of course."

"Yes, my name is from the land. As am I, originally," said Elizabeth.

"No! How can that be?" Zethar thought they were joking at first. But there were some physical differences between Elizabeth and all the other maids she knew—darker skin, a different shape to her eyes, and an outline to her tail fin more akin to that of a merman.

"As I might take a land-man to be my husband, so I chose to take a land-woman as my maidwife," said Saraid. "The same change that befalls land-men happens to their women too, but with one great difference. Elizabeth has not declined over the years. She has not suffered the Dark Change, which robs maids of their husbands, even after ten years among us."

Zethar marvelled at this and considered how little she actually knew of the world. Among her own clan, she was well-educated, but here her eyes were opened to new wonders and possibilities. The merfolk here were constantly impressed with her ability to see into other's bodies, and it wasn't long before she was able to use the talent to help with healing a persistent injury sustained by one of the hunters.

Rhian was curious as to how she had found out about the existence of the clan. Zethar recounted Senara's story of her time here, and Rhian nodded at some of the details.

"It was before my time," she said, "but my mother told me of the great nets that destroyed our habitations. That was when we developed these dwellings you see here today—made from fabrics stolen from the land. They are not natural animal skins but crafted by some magic of the land-folk."

Zethar nodded. "I have seen them make such houses near the beaches of my home waters. They unfold them, sit in them for days when it rains, shouting and arguing, their children crying, then fold them up and take them away. I have never understood the purpose."

"In truth, there are some mysteries of the land-folk we may never understand. Such a pity Elizabeth can no longer remember her time with them."

The fishers would often venture close in to shore to collect the shellfish that proliferated in the shallows. One day Zethar went with them, keen to get a close look at the land bordering her new home. As they approached, Tavie spoke a warning.

"Stay low when you surface. The beach here is often crawling with land-folk. It's safe to go as far as the back edge of those rocks, but no further."

Zethar heeded the advice and took care not to be seen, reaching her arms out to pluck the tastiest molluscs she came across without rising out of the water. Taking a breath in the shelter of a rock she thought would give her cover, she rested and surveyed the view towards the land. Only after thirty seconds or so did she become aware of a girl, no more than four years old, standing on the rocks nearby, staring directly at her, mouth hanging open.

"Ashwin!" yelled the girl. "Come and see! A mermaid!"

Zethar exhaled and dived quickly with a splash of her grey tail. From under the water, she could see the girl scanning the surface where she had been. An older boy joined her, also peering down.

"You are such a liar, Priya," he said. "There's nothing here."

"But there was... I *saw* her," protested the girl, as she followed her brother back towards the beach. Zethar giggled to herself but then felt sorry for the tiny girl, whom nobody would believe. Saraid swam up beside her.

"Do be careful!" she said. "There are many of them on the beach now. We'd better head back."

With pouches full of mussels, whelks, and limpets, the maids returned to deeper waters.

****

The days became weeks and the weeks became months, but Zethar didn't fret over the passage of time. Although she missed her family and friends far away to the south, so the new life she had found kept her busy and provided satisfaction. They were a smaller group than the Kernow clan, numbering around twenty-two, but their territory stretched many miles north and south, and out into the deep sea. There was no sudden drop off in this region, more of a gentle slope down, and the area available for farming was increased. Because of this, the fields were not so intensively tended. With such a wide area to gather from, the clan never worried about going hungry.

Zethar learned the art of net weaving, the techniques of fishing, and the basics of using the hunting spear. She had to admit she had no exceptional skill at any of these tasks and was glad she had spent her earlier years studying the healing arts and rituals of the merfolk. Those skills were also in demand here, for although most maids knew the basics of treating simple conditions, none had her deep knowledge.

More than a year passed before Zethar realised she hadn't thought of her previous life for a couple of days. She was happy here with her new friends. She could never go back, but she no longer felt the need to.

CHAPTER SEVEN
Homecoming

One day, nearly two years after she had joined the Candtowan, Zethar was preparing to fish in deep waters with Tavie. They had readied their nets and were setting off when a couple of other maids called out nearby. Gwylan swooped down from the surface, spear at the ready in case of danger.

"What's going on?" called Rhian.

"Something's coming. I don't know what," replied Gwylan. "Everyone should be on their guard."

Then there came a shout from someone towards the edge of the home crater.

"It's a maid! A stranger in our waters."

Gwylan dashed over to get a better look, her streaked hair flowing straight behind her. A couple of other maids rose up and went with her. Zethar craned to look from where she was, but the water wasn't clear enough to see from this distance. She too swam forward towards the others.

Approaching from the south was a figure swimming at immense speed. She was still far away, but Zethar's heart jumped as she recognised the visitor. Or rather, one of two people it could be. Only when the maid came close enough to make out the spiral tattoos on her torso could she be certain which twin it was.

"Tamon!" she cried, speeding forward to meet her sister. Tamon looked tired. She'd clearly been swimming with all her might to get here, but the look of joy spreading across her face on seeing Zethar wiped away the exhaustion. They grabbed each other in a tight hug.

"Zethi, it's so good to find you! My... you look well. How have you been?"

Before Zethar could answer, Gwylan approached.

"Who is this? You two know each other?" she asked, examining Tamon closely.

"This is my sister, Tamon."

"Your sister? Ah, I see the resemblance now," said Gwylan. "Any of your family are welcome guests. I apologise for our cautious greeting."

"No offence taken," said Tamon. "I'm pleased to have found you. I have been swimming at speed for two days and most of the night."

"Then you will be in need of rest," Zethar said. "Come down with me and have something to eat."

Gwylan went to inform Rhian who the visitor was, and the two sisters swam over to a comfortable sand bank below an overhang of the petrified circle. Zethar fetched some fresh plaice, which Tamon devoured quickly.

"Oh, I needed that." The copper-haired maid stretched out on the sand, resting from her hard swim.

"It's so wonderful you're here. I thought I'd never see you again. How is Mother? And Kensa and Kerra? And Delen? And—"

"They're fine. All of them," Tamon interrupted. "They all wanted to come with me, in fact, but as the swiftest swimmer, I was the logical choice to go alone. I am fortunate to have found you so easily. And I was so worried you might not be here. Not a day goes by when we don't think of you."

A sudden thought hit Zethar. "Wait... aren't you all forbidden from seeking me out, as I am forbidden to return?"

"Yes. That's true. But there's a problem the clan needs your help with. My arrival here is not purely from missing you."

"A problem? Affecting everyone?"

"Well... it's more, um..." Tamon hesitated. "It's really Rozen who needs your help."

"Rozen? She can forget it." Zethar folded her arms and clenched her tail. "She had me thrown out of my home, and I don't see why I should flick a fin to help that maid."

"Precisely because she had you thrown out. That's why we thought you should help her."

This made no sense to Zethar, but Tamon clarified her meaning.

"Rozen took a husband a year ago, is pregnant," she said, "and the baby is due soon. But something is wrong. She keeps experiencing great pain, in a way no other maid who has borne children can understand. As the single wise one of our clan now, Rozen herself cannot find a cure for it. When the pain comes, it leaves her weak, and it increases each time. There is a worry she may die—and her unborn daughter with her."

Zethar scowled. "Let her feel pain. Let her feel the pain she inflicted on my heart with her lies. I care not."

"But what about the baby? Is it right that she may suffer too, or even die from whatever ails her mother?"

"No... I suppose not. She is innocent, whoever her mother is."

"There is more to it," Tamon said, "and it may benefit you. As your accuser, Rozen was responsible for your exile. Only one thing can end the sentence and allow your return—Rozen's forgiveness. If you can help her, I am sure she will be grateful and might call for your exile to end."

Could it be true?

Zethar's stomach gave a flutter at the idea. Though she hated Rozen, she could not really sit by and let her and the baby suffer. Her duty as a healer had to come first, and fate had given her the skill and talent to be of use. And if she could truly come back...

"All right. I will help her."

Tamon smiled and clasped her sister's hand. "You are doing the right thing. And Mother will be so delighted to see you!"

****

Later that evening, Rhian took Zethar aside. The Candtowan had made Tamon welcome and provided a good meal for her, and while she chatted to curious members of the clan, Rhian wanted to have a private word with Zethar.

"I know you have a strong tie to your family. I don't want to stand in the way of that," said Rhian. "But you know me... I speak plainly, and I can't help but say what worries me. I fear you will leave us for good if you return to help the pregnant maid. You are truly one of us, and so many here care about you."

Zethar nodded slowly, considering Rhian's words.

"It's possible. I miss my mother and sisters greatly. I'd forgotten how much until Tamon came. I have such good friends here, though—I don't know what I'd do, to be honest."

"Zethar, I'd be lying if I didn't admit that we like having you with us for your own sake. You're always so lively and cheerful and you lift our spirits every day. But equally, you bring so much knowledge to us. Nobody here can match your healing skills. You're exceptional."

Rhian's eyes conveyed her plea as much as her words did. Zethar thought for a moment before replying.

"Yes. I do have a talent. But that's why I *must* go."

Disappointment was obvious on Rhian's face.

"You're right," she said. "It is a good thing to do. I understand."

****

Three days later, Tamon and Zethar reached the Sacred Rocks, two enormous islands of stone rising up from the water. They marked the boundary of the clan's territory and Zethar truly was back home again. They turned west and soon the village came in sight. Maids and men turned to look at Zethar with surprise, not expecting to see her.

"Did you tell anyone I was coming?" muttered Zethar.

"Hmm, not outside the family... in case there was resistance to the idea."

"You do realise that means I might get stuck with a spear, don't you?"

Tamon winked. "Not with the strongest hunter in the ocean beside you, you won't."

But it was soon apparent this claim was to be tested. Before the pair reached the caves, their path was blocked by two burly men with weapons at the ready. One was Ciaran, the other a man whom Zethar didn't recognise.

"Zethar! You mustn't return here," commanded Ciaran, astonished to see her. "I cannot permit you to enter the caves."

"She's here to help Rozen. If you stop her, you deny a mother-to-be her chance of safe delivery," said Tamon. Ciaran hesitated and lowered his spear a little, but the other man continued to point his trident at Zethar. With complete calm, Tamon swam between her sister and the guard and put her hand on the tines of the trident.

"Henry," she said, "unless you want to have these spikes stuck through your chest, you will let us pass." She pushed the trident aside and glared. Henry remained in place, looking determined. But Ciaran spoke up.

"She's not making an idle threat. I think we should let them through."

Zethar wasn't sure if she imagined a trace of admiration at her sister's bravery in Ciaran's voice. Henry swam aside and the maids continued on their way.

They entered the caves and swam through to the small side chamber where Rozen rested—the same one Morveren had occupied when Zethar was a baby. The pregnant maid was asleep, but stirred on hearing them enter. Her eyes flicked open wide.

"Zethar? It's you! Why are you here? How dare you come back. I shall call for a hunter to pierce your heart this instant!"

"Oh, a fine welcome for your one-time friend," said Tamon. "It is on *my* request she is here, and before you have her thrown out, listen to my reasons."

"Very well," said Rozen, although she didn't look any happier.

"You are suffering, and even you think there is a risk you and your daughter could die."

"That is true." Rozen stroked her round belly.

"Zethar knows the healing arts, as you do. But she has the Song of the Dolphin, and she can see right inside you. She can see—in a way nobody else can—what is happening in your body to cause this pain. And maybe then she can do something to ease it."

Rozen pulled a sulky face as she mulled this idea over.

"I don't like the thought of her looking at the inside of my body. It isn't normal," she said. Tamon sighed.

"Oh, Rozen, be reasonable! You can let Zethi use her talent, or you can let her swim back to her new home and leave you in agony. The choice is yours." Tamon turned and left the pair of them alone in the chamber to decide.

Clearly, the thought of continued pain was too much for Rozen. "I suppose it is the only way I might be helped. Zethar, will you do what you can for me... please?"

Zethar nodded. "I will. Now, stretch out... That's good."

She placed her head on the other maid's abdomen,

resting against the taut skin with gentle pressure. She began a steady hum, increasing in intensity, and as she closed her eyes the structures beneath the skin became apparent.

There was the baby, her tail coiled up over her shoulder. She moved slightly, flexing her fin. A ball of fluid surrounded the tiny maid, her own miniature sea, and around this were the life-giving vessels carrying Rozen's blood, flowing to the cord which anchored baby and mother together. Zethar could even see the movement of blood through the cord.

As she watched, the baby stirred again, straightening her tail. Rozen cried out. The baby's tail was pushing down on a knot of blood vessels, blocking them off temporarily. That was what caused the pain. If the baby continued to do this, she might not only harm Rozen but herself, as she would restrict her own supply.

"I know what the problem is," said Zethar, lifting her head up. "Your daughter is in a bad position. Her tail is down, her head is up."

"She should be the other way round," said Rozen.

"When she moves her tail, it's pushing on the vessels feeding the cord. We must turn her around."

Rozen's pasty face went even paler. "No! It's too difficult. Senara told us it stands a good chance of killing the baby, remember?"

"Senara didn't have an advantage that I do. She couldn't see the baby while turning her. And if we don't turn her, she will likely die during birth anyway."

Zethar instructed Rozen to swim into a position with her head down and tail up then told her to stay like that for a while.

"Where in the ocean did you learn this strange method?" asked the uncomfortable mother-to-be.

"From one of the maids in the Candtowan clan. They know many things about childbirth Senara never taught us. Just trust me."

Zethar ducked under Rozen's body and took a quick look inside her again. The baby had not budged from her position, but had at least drawn her tail back against herself.

"Right, this isn't working. I will need to push her."

Rozen gave Zethar a worried look as she turned over and lay on her back. Zethar positioned her hands carefully on the bump, all the time glancing inside to check she was lining up correctly. Pressing in the wrong place could easily damage the baby's tail, with fatal results.

"This may hurt a bit."

The scream from Rozen was unexpected and terribly loud. Zethar didn't mean to hurt her, but she needed to press firmly. Inside her mother, the baby squirmed and resisted Zethar's pressure, as if annoyed to be moved from her comfortable resting place.

"I can't take this!" whimpered Rozen.

"Yes, you can. It won't be for long... She's wriggling again."

"I know. I can... ah... feel it!"

The baby twisted her shoulders, squirmed her tail, then flipped right round, her head downwards in Rozen's narrow pelvis, and her tail upwards where it could no longer press on anything vital. Rozen gave another loud shout as this happened, then relaxed. After a moment she surfaced and took a deep gulp of air from the bubble inside the chamber.

"How are you feeling now?" asked Zethar.

"Like I've been punched in the gut," said Rozen, brushing strands of blonde hair from her face, "but it's less of an acute pain than it was. More of a dull ache."

"That should ease soon. She is the right way round now. And by the way, she looks absolutely beautiful."

Rozen actually smiled. "Thank you for saying so. And... thank you for helping me. Nobody else could have done the turning, you know. I am in your debt."

"Well, what you decide to do is up to you, as Tamon

said. I'll let you rest a while now." Leaving her hint hanging, Zethar swam out into the main chamber. It was time to catch up with her family.

****

Zethar had never seen her mother so delighted as when she arrived at the kelp fields to greet her. Kensa was there too, and they swamped Zethar in their happy embrace.

"Tamon told me she'd found you, but I didn't want to disturb you while you dealt with Rozen," Morveren said. "You are looking so... wise and grown up now!"

Kensa rolled her eyes. "She looks just the same, Mother, apart from she's tied her hair up differently."

"You haven't changed either, Kensa!" said Zethar with a laugh. "And where is my third sister today?"

"Oh, probably out on the beach again. She's hanging around on land so much these days I'm sure she will grow legs," said Kensa

"Don't be mean, dear," said Morveren. "You know she has taken a fancy to a land-man. Kerra will have her husband before long, I dare say."

Zethar stayed with them until their work among the kelp was done then all three swam back to the caves. Kerra had returned from her excursion and whooped with joy when she saw her sister. The family ate together and Zethar told tales of what she'd been up to over the last two years.

"I'd not believe it, if I'd not seen the clan with my own eyes," said Tamon. "The way they make their own houses rather than using caves… it's extraordinary."

After they had eaten, the family had a couple more visitors.

"May I intrude upon you?" asked Rozen. She was accompanied by a handsome merman. "Zethar, I'd like you to meet my husband, Timothy." Timothy bowed low in greeting.

"I cannot thank you enough for what you did for Roz today. I was afraid I would lose both my wife and our daughter," he said.

"I was glad to do it. To make a positive difference and help people... that is my purpose in life. It's what I strive for."

"Zethar, can I speak to you in private?" Rozen looked nervous.

"Of course." She went out into a side passage and Rozen followed.

"I don't expect you to forgive me," the blonde maid began, "but I want you to know I truly believe I was wrong about you. When you came to help me—*me*, of all people, who had you cast out into the open sea—I realised there was no way you could have done any harm to Senara. I didn't see the real you back then. Now I have, and I am humbled. You have a good heart, Zethar, and I wish I hadn't been cruel to you. Jealousy of your talent made me hate it but without it, my daughter might never be born."

Zethar was surprised to hear such a heartfelt confession from her, and she could tell the words were genuine.

"Will you return to us from your exile?" Rozen asked.

Zethar looked about her. This village had once contained her whole life. She thought of the open spaces where she had swam and played as a little girl, the sandy beaches at the edge of the land, all the people she knew and loved from growing up.

They were all here. But they would always be here, and now she noticed a twinge of homesickness for another place. She shook her head.

"I have a new life now, and that is where I will be happiest. I shall stay a few days, and I will always return here... but it's not my home anymore."

Morveren begged her daughter to change her mind when she broke the news she would be returning to her home in the north, but she understood. It was hard for a mother to let her daughter go, but easier when it was her daughter's own choice.

"I will come back, at least every season," she promised. "I won't forget you!"

The future lay before her, like the ocean itself—infinite and as yet unseen. Would she travel again, perhaps to the lochs of the far north or the warm currents of southern seas? Would she meet a land-man and bear daughters of her own?

Zethar swished her tail, gave one last fond wave to her loved ones, and went to find out.

-Fin-

APPENDIX: THE MERMAID GUIDE

Air Caves
The merfolk breathe air, as do all other sea going mammals, but they also need protection while they sleep. Their solution is to find underwater caves, either with natural air pockets or where they can bring bubbles of air down to create such spaces. When air caves are not available, merfolk are forced to sleep at the surface. However, the Candtowan clan found their own solution by making primitive underwater tents. The air caves are illuminated by little phosphorescent organisms brought up from deep waters.

Athina
As far as is known, Athina is the only child of Kerra by her husband Jonathan. Athina is graceful, with long blonde hair, green eyes and green spiral tattoos on her torso. She is nineteen when we meet her in *Deep Secrets*. It is not known what Athina's role in the clan is, but the tattoos she bears are simple decorations and not marks of status *(see Tamon)*. It is from Athina that we learn that mermaids cannot read or write the languages of the land, despite being able to speak them. She seeks out her half brother Toby partly from curiosity and partly from a desire to have him explain a message left by their father. Unusually, Athina's name is not Cornish but is of Greek origin.

Basking shark
The world's second-largest shark species, *Cetorhinus maximus* is a harmless plankton eater that is often sighted in the waters around Britain.

Bawden Rocks
These two stony islands rising from the sea mark one of the outer boundaries of the Kernow clan's territory. They

call them the Sacred Rocks, and it is in the hollow interior of the larger one where Jonathan Moore leaves a message for his son. In reality, the rocks are not hollow, and neither do they have the treacherous currents around them described in *Deep Secrets*. They lie off the coast a little way from St Agnes. The beach that Athina and Toby set out from (and return to) when they visit the rocks is actually Trevaunance Cove.

Cailplena
The merfolk's name for the sea potato weed, *Leathesia difformis*. They use it as an anti-inflammatory medicine and also to staunch bleeding. It is ground into a sticky paste and applied to the skin.

Chadwick, Fritz
An undergraduate student at the university, with brown curly hair and a goatee beard. Fritz is a friend of Toby Moore and also assists him with his work for the MMS in his spare time. He lusts after his university course supervisor, Abbie Lindridge. Fritz often jokes around, which grates on Toby. His frustration at feeling left out when Athina is captured, combined with his attraction to Professor Lindridge, leads him to make plans which undermine Toby.

Cherryson, Rob
One of those people who thinks they are funnier than they really are, the jovial Rob worked with Jonathan Moore at Mayfield Labs. He is in his forties, with a beard and greying curly hair. After the events in *The Maid of Trelanton* he goes to work for NASA in California.

Ciaran
A hunter of the Kernow clan, Ciaran has blond curly hair and a muscular physique. He has a casual friendship with Zethar and her sisters and admires Tamon's bravery as a

hunter. Ciaran represents his profession on the council that presides over Zethar's trial. Presumably he has a maidwife, but she is never identified

Dark Change

This is the merfolk's name for the mental deterioration suffered by all mermen. Once they have been taken from the land and completed their transformation, they will suffer the Dark Change at any time from two to six years later. Most experience it at about three or four years. The merman will develop confusion, memory problems, mood swings and an inability to recognise the members of his clan. Eventually he will dive too deeply to return for air, and meet death by drowning. It appears that land-women can transform into mermaids without suffering this deterioration *(see Elizabeth)*. Although it's not specifically referred to as such anywhere in the Trelanton Tales, the process by which a land-man becomes a merman is known as the Bright Change. Its effect is described by Kerra in *The Maid of Trelanton*, and as well as the physical changes that allow a man to survive under the sea, it also involves a certain amount of memory loss. It can be concluded from this that the message Jonathan leaves for his son in *Deep Secrets* was written before this change was fully effected.

Delen

Only sister of Morveren, and aunt to her children. Delen has no offspring of her own, despite having had a husband. We do not know his name, only that he lived just two years before undergoing the Dark Change. Her occupation is weaver. The name is Cornish and means 'petal'.

Demelza's Cafe

Priya's place of employment in Porthleven. Its scones are as legendary as its sea views.

Elizabeth
A land-woman who was taken to join the merfolk when she became the maidwife of Saraid. Unlike land-men, Elizabeth hasn't suffered the Dark Change, even after ten years as a mermaid. She did, however, lose her memory of life on land as men do. Her appearance differs from natural born mermaids in that her skin is darker, her tail shape is different and her eyes are not quite the same as those of other maids.

Gwylan
A member of the Candtowan who is the first to encounter Zethar. She prefers to spend much of her time hunting and has a fierce demeanour, although her voice is soft. Her hair is pale blonde with brown streaks running through it. Her name means 'seagull' in Welsh and was a deliberate choice to mirror her Cornish counterpart.

Henry
A merman who challenges Zethar when she returns home after her exile. He is a hunter of the clan.

Isur
The merfolk's name for the shark *Isurus oxyrinchus*, commonly known as the shortfin mako. These sharks are very seldom seen near Cornwall, but it's not beyond the bounds of possibility that the merfolk there might encounter one. In a slightly ironic twist, although Tamon is awarded the accolade of Swordfish for killing an isur in *Seagull's Exile*, in reality the swordfish is one of the shark's preferred foods.

Kensa
Eldest daughter of Morveren (by a few minutes over her identical twin Tamon) and sister of Kerra and Zethar. When we first meet Kensa she is just five years old. In her adult life she is a farmer like her mother. She has red hair

and brown eyes and a more gentle nature than her twin, although she is moved to violence when assisting in the capture of Toby Moore. The name means 'first' in Cornish, reflecting her status as the elder twin. The copper toned hair of the sisters came about from a friend's suggestion that there should be more ginger mermaids!

Kerra

The mermaid after whom *The Maid of Trelanton* is titled. The mother of Athina, daughter of Morveren, maidwife of Jonathan, sister of Kensa, Tamon and Zethar. She has very dark grey hair, brown eyes, and wears a necklace of slender seaweed. Her role in the clan is farming, although most of her appearances in the stories take place on the shore. She is the only mermaid to be seen in all three tales. She makes jewellery as a hobby, and this includes the seaweed bracelet she gives to Jonathan Moore on their first proper meeting. At that time she is aged twenty-four, although she is just three at the start of *Seagull's Exile* and around forty-seven when we see her in *Deep Secrets*. Her name means 'dearest' (and Morveren addresses her as such in the story).

Kittiwake

A adorable little seagull, *Rissa tridactyla*. They are widespread, and nest on sheer cliffs. The kittiwake colony at Porthcurno was the inspiration for their inclusion at the fictional Trelanton Cove.

Languages

In *The Maid of Trelanton* and *Deep Secrets*, the mermaids speak to the land-folk in English, which they have picked up from hearing their speech over many years. Mermaids in the seas of other countries learn languages of the lands nearby, so French mermaids can speak French, and so on. Although they speak it, we learn in the second story that they can't read or write it The merfolk's own language developed underwater, and lacks many of the sounds commonly used in terrestrial language. Conversely, it includes many sounds almost never used above the surface but which transmit well through water, such as clicks and hums. To our ears, it would sound like strange mumbling.

Lindridge, Abigail

Professor Abigail Lindridge (known as Abbie) was Toby Moore's course supervisor when he was at university and is now supervising Fritz Chadwick. Her field is marine biology and it is to her that Fritz brings the injured Athina. Her appearance is never described but presumably she is quite attractive, and Fritz's photographs reveal that she sunbathes topless.

Marine Monitoring Service (MMS)

A fictional organisation involved in marine research in the waters around the British Isles. Toby Moore works for them, tagging basking sharks.

Mayfield Labs

Employers of Jonathan Moore and Rob Cherryson. The labs house an anechoic chamber where the scientists test the acoustic properties of different materials.

Minnarin

A seaweed extract used as a painkiller by the merfolk. It is placed in the mouth and absorbed there.

Moore, Anna

Anna is the wife of Jonathan Moore and mother of Toby Moore. She hails from Donegal, in the Republic of Ireland. She is rather self centred and does not realise how her obsession with caring for baby Toby is pushing her husband away from her. Although Jonathan leaves a note telling her he is going to live with a mermaid, Anna refuses to believe it, thinking her husband has psychological issues. She has brown curly hair.

Moore, Jonathan

A scientist in the field of acoustic research, Jonathan worked at Mayfield Labs in Cornwall, alongside Rob Cherryson. He is married to Anna and has a baby son, Toby. He is of medium build, has light brown hair and is aged thirty. He meets Kerra at Trelanton Cove and falls in love with her, eventually abandoning his life on land to be with her under the sea. After that we hear about him only through the accounts of his wife and daughter and from the message he writes for Toby. *The Maid of Trelanton* is told from his point of view.

Moore, Toby

The main protagonist of *Deep Secrets*, we first meet Toby as a baby in *The Maid of Trelanton*. His parents are Jonathan and Anna Moore. As a twenty-three year old he works as a marine biologist, tagging basking sharks. Ambitious and a little full of himself, his encounter with his half sister Athina changes his feelings about his father. An expert surfer, Toby has stereotypical 'surf dude' looks with shaggy blonde hair.

Morveren

Mother of Kensa, Tamon, Kerra and Zethar and maidwife of Pierre. Morveren's physical appearance is never actually described, but she is a caring and gentle maid who loves her family above all else. Her role in the clan is as a farmer. The name comes from the Cornish legend about the mermaid of Zennor, possibly the most famous mermaid story in the area. A mermaid called Morveren used to attend the church at Zennor to hear the singing of Mathew (or Mathey) Trewella, and ended up seducing him to live under the sea with her.

Mullion
The harbour where Toby and Fritz base their shark tagging operation, and the site of the MMS warehouse, is at Mullion. This village is on the south coast of Cornwall, facing out into Mount's Bay. The picturesque harbour is a notable tourist attraction.

Pierre
Never appears directly in the stories, but is talked about and remembered by other maids. Pierre is the husband of Morveren and father of Kensa, Tamon, Kerra and Zethar. He survived as a merman for six years before succumbing to the Dark Change during his wife's third pregnancy, and dies at about the same time Zethar is born. Nothing is known of his previous life on land or how Morveren came to meet him. We do know that he had brown eyes and that his daughters resemble him in certain characteristics. Kerra has no memory of him by the time she reaches adulthood, although according to her, Kensa and Tamon do remember him.

Porthleven
The opening scene of *Deep Secrets* is set on this renowned surfing beach, which gets the waves coming in from Mount's Bay. It really does have some very challenging surf conditions at times.

Raoul
Raoul is a merman who travelled to Kernow from the Mediterranean. His back story is chronicled in an as yet unreleased tale called *The Mermaid's Kiss*. Suffice to say, having lost his maidwife he travelled northwards and ended up romantically involved with Rozen. After suffering a shark bite injury he takes a fancy to Zethar and makes a pass at her, which ultimately leads to the rift between Zethar and Rozen. This also results in the disintegration of his relationship with Rozen.

Rhian
The leader of the Candtowan clan, Rhian has black hair adorned with a coral circlet, and is very beautiful. She is generally friendly and appreciates the talents of those in her clan.

Rozen
Somewhat cocky and headstrong, Rozen is the best friend of Zethar and, like her, one of Senara's acolytes. A pretty maid with blonde hair, Rozen suffers from a streak of jealousy which disrupts her friendship with Zethar. Rozen has a romantic relationship with Raoul, but this does not last, and a few years later she takes Timothy as a husband and becomes pregnant by him. Her pregnancy does not go smoothly and she reluctantly accepts help from Zethar. Her name means 'rose' in Cornish, although it's unlikely mermaids would ever see roses!

Sacred Rocks
See: Bawden Rocks

Saraid
A mermaid from Scotland who now lives with the Candtowan clan in Cardigan Bay. Best friends with Tavie, and maidwife to Elizabeth.

Senara
The oldest of the Kernow clan, Senara is their wise one – a role encompassing that of healer, priestess and teacher. She takes on Rozen and Zethar as her acolytes. She was born somewhere off the west coast of Ireland, then travelled to join the Candtowan clan in Cardigan Bay, and later arrived in Kernow. Her hair is mostly white by the time we meet her in the story, and she is the only mermaid to be seen to die. Her name comes from St Senara, patron saint of the village of Zennor *(see Morveren)*.

Sharma, Ashwin
Priya's elder brother, who does not believe in mermaids.

Sharma, Priya
Toby Moore's girlfriend. She works as a waitress at Demelza's Cafe. Generally bubbly and affectionate, she has secretly believed in mermaids ever since spotting Zethar from the beach when she was just a little girl. She owns a cat, but its name is unknown. She has long black hair and is aged twenty-six.

The Shelf
This is the point at which the shallow coastal waters around Cornwall drop down to the depths of the Atlantic, beyond which the merfolk rarely venture. For plot purposes I made this region very much closer to the coast than it is in reality.

Song of the Dolphin
The ability to 'see' using ultrasonic waves, much as whales and dolphins do. A very rare talent among the merfolk and one possessed by Zethar. The skill enables a maid to find their position by echolocation in an enclosed space, spot objects with differing reflective properties, and also to observe the interior structures of living creatures, as medical ultrasound does.

Stensow
The word for 'crab' in the language of the merfolk. It is loosely based on a Cornish translation meaning 'stone louse'. Mermaids find them notoriously difficult to draw.

Tamon
Daughter of Morveren, younger identical twin of Kensa, and elder sister of Kerra and Zethar. Although sharing her twin's looks, Tamon is the bolder and more aggressive of

the two. She makes her first appearance at five years old and her last aged roughly forty-nine, when she assists in capturing Toby Moore. Tamon is distinguishable from Kensa by her tattooed body, which she acquired on achieving the hunting accolade of Swordfish. She shows no fear and has a fierce loyalty to her family. Her name means 'sea pink' in Cornish, the plant also known as thrift, which is described as growing around the fringes of Trelanton Cove.

Tavie
A mermaid from Scotland now resident with the Candtowan. She travelled there with Saraid and Elizabeth.

Timothy
Husband of Rozen and father of her unborn daughter, Timothy joins the clan some time after Zethar is exiled. His social role is unknown.

Tom
Tom is the university security guard, on good terms with Toby Moore from the latter's student days. His surname is not known. He has a wife called Melissa.

Trelanton Cove
A beach frequented by the merfolk. It is here that Jonathan Moore meets Kerra, and it is also the site the clan use for their sacred ceremonies. It lies on the north coast of Cornwall. It's not actually a real place, but the beach which it is based on can be found on the stretch of coast midway between Gwithian and Portreath.

Tressa
A friend of Kerra and Rozen, Tressa never appears directly but it is she who gossips to Rozen about Zethar's kiss with Raoul. The name is Cornish for 'third' so presumably she has two elder sisters somewhere.

The University

This is where Toby gained his degree in marine biology and where Fritz currently studies under the tutelage of Professor Lindridge. It's not specified exactly where the university is. It is a fictional entity and not based on any real Cornish higher education institutions.

Zethar

Youngest daughter of Morveren, sister of Kensa, Tamon and Kerra. Zethar's life up to the age of twenty-one is chronicled in *Seagull's Exile*, but what happens to her after that is unknown. She has chestnut brown hair and wears a necklace of small stones and shells. Her most notable feature is her ability to 'see' using ultrasonic waves, an ability known as the Song of the Dolphin by the merfolk. Though intelligent, Zethar is rather naive and timid at times. As mentioned in the story, her name really does mean 'seagull' in Cornish, for her ability to mimic the birds.

ACKNOWLEDGEMENTS

I would like to thank several people who helped me take my mermaids a step closer to reality. Matt Drzymała, George Bourdaniotis and Pip Sprake for their encouragement during my first steps into writing, Louisa Brown for guidance in finding a publisher, Jamie Rose for her thorough polishing of my words, Juliette Dodd for her beautiful artwork, Nicki Osman and Lauren Head for defining the ultimate mermaid (and what she should eat), and my wife Monika and daughter Juliette for being patient with me while I wrote.

ABOUT THE AUTHOR

Simon Peel lives in the English seaside town of Hastings, with his family and an assortment of animals. When he's not writing he enjoys playing guitar and keyboards, photography, and sleeping. He is always happy to hear from readers and can be contacted at audiodentist@hotmail.com.

Printed in Great Britain
by Amazon